MOON DAUGHTER'S FATE

AUTHOR:
Alice Peng

EDITORS:
Jeff Harkness, Matt Finch

SUBSTANTIVE EDITOR:
Brandon Powers

PATHFINDER CONVERSION:
Michael Mars Russell

ART DIRECTOR:
Casey Christofferson

LAYOUT:
Suzy Moseby

INTERIOR ART:
Santa Norvaisaite, Adrian Landeros

CARTOGRAPHY:
Robert Altbauer

FRONT COVER ART:
Michael Syrigos

COVER DESIGN:
Casey Christofferson

NECROMANCER Games

ISBN: 978-1-6656-0018-7
PF PoD

Table of Contents

By Alice Peng

An adventure for for 4–6 characters of levels 5–8

Chapter One : Introduction

This adventure by Alice Peng is suitable for 4–6 characters of levels 5–8, and is located in a fictional, folkloric region of China. If the gaming group is using existing characters, the means by which they reach the Whisper Valley is best determined by the context of their prior adventures.

Overview

The setup for this adventure begins with the characters discovering a provincial roadhouse where a terrible attack occurred, during which a young woman was taken. The situation is, however, one of considerable significance. A powerful deity of the region was trapped during the battle and still lingers in a state of poison-induced madness. The characters must track down the missing woman and help restore the balance to the land before an evil cult (and the force behind their power) can cause widespread devastation.

Because the land's balance has been thrown off, another deity, Leigong (God of Thunder, Smiter of Evil) has become involved, and identified the characters as a possible solution to the existing problem. Their encounter with Leigong marks the beginning of the adventure.

Reading the Adventure

The first appearance of each name in this adventure contains a guide to its tonal pronunciation.

The pronunciation of a syllable is designated with a number: 1, 2, 3, 4, or none.

1. A high tone, a tone used in English when someone sounds surprised.

2. Goes from down to up and sounds a bit like a question mark would follow it.

3. Goes from down to up. Rather than sounding like a question mark, this is a more extended syllable.

4. Goes from up to down. Sometimes it can sound like someone's adding an exclamation point to their word or sound almost a little angry.

5. No number is a common sentence ender with no true equivalent in English. The word is pronounced extremely quickly and drops in the second half of the syllable.

Adventure Start

The adventure begins when the characters encounter the disguised god *Lei2Gong1* (Leigong) on the road to the city of *Wei4Feng1* (Weifeng, "Reason's Wind"), and they are most likely diverted from the main road to a smaller, more rural route. It is relatively clear from the encounter with Leigong that an adventure lies along the rural path, and the characters have no pressing business in Weifeng. While there are clues in Leigong's appearance to his identity, the characters will only know him as an old man.

The mandates and rules of heaven outline acceptable actions for gods meddling and interacting with the world of mortals. This often prevents gods from taking direct action unless within a specific domain.

For example, Leigong can punish someone by striking them down with lightning but his lightning can't penetrate into many locations so he must use mortals to handle the situation.

Leigong is a Chinese Taoist deity known as the "Duke of Thunder" or "Thunder God." Heaven mandated him to punish mortals and spirits alike that used their knowledge of Taoism to commit evil acts. His deific depictions often have him with claws, bat or red-feathered wings, an axe or hammer, a chisel, and a set of drums.

The Encounter with Leigong

Read or summarize the following information to the players, adding whatever transition you feel is necessary from their prior adventures:

The province of *Sheng1Xi1Gu3* (Sheng Xi Gu, "Whisper Valley") is flanked by two high mountains to the northwest and southeast, and bounded by hills to the northeast and southwest with the *Bi4Jiang1* (Bi Jiang, "Silk River") flowing through. Abundant in agriculture, coal, and trade, Shen Xi Gu is a wealthy and metropolitan province with major trade routes passing through the hills bounding the ends of the province.

You are traveling to the metropolitan city of Weifeng over hilly country for the late-summer *Qi1xi1* (Qixi, "The Night of Sevens") holiday festivities. You are not pursuing any mission in particular, but you are looking forward to the festival.

Along the road, however, you run into a strange encounter.

Any character with some kind of divine attunement can get a sense that the man might be more than he appears to be. Characters who roll a successful DC 15 Knowledge (religion) check can connect the symbolism in his winged robe and axe to Leigong but should not be able to make any overt connections.

Read or summarize the following information to the players.

This is the god Leigong in human guise. He pretends to be a simple man cutting firewood and will introduce himself as Lei2Lao3Ye (Old Man Lei —Lei2 can be interpreted as simply a common surname but that same word also happens to mean Thunder). Leigong is manipulating weather and terrain in the hopes that the characters' natures will incline them to go where Leigong is unable to.

Assuming that the characters engage him in conversation, he informs them that the road ahead is washed out, and that if they are on their way to Weifeng, they might be delayed if they plan to arrive in time for the Qixi festivities. He does, however, tell them that they already passed another way to the city only half a mile back. It is longer, but now that the main road is washed out, it is probably still the quicker path. It is also, he says rather enigmatically, the "better" path.

The characters can continue to talk with Leigong, but the mandates and rules of Heaven (see Side Box) prevent him from giving them any further useful information. The only other thing he will say if asked for further information, and it is of as-yet-unknown significance is: "Well, I'm chopping wood, you are on the road to Weifeng, and the price of coal seems to be going up in Mei Zhen." If the characters ask about Mei Zhen, he will tell them that it's a coal-mining town that can be reached on the smaller turn-off behind them. Beyond this, he gives them no further information, saying that he has to get back to his work.

BACKGROUND

Nearly two decades ago, *Qing2Shan1* (Qing Shan, "Passionate Mountain") fled execution for becoming pregnant before marriage. Fearing to be caught, she avoided cities and towns, but a group of bandits attacked her on the road, leaving her for dead. A traveling monk discovered her and brought her back to the provincial roadhouse he managed, where he witnessed the birth of Qing Shan's daughter, *Hua4Yue4* (Hua Yue, "Tranquil Moon"). After the monk died, Qing Shan has been the caretaker of the roadhouse with the assistance of her daughter.

Bandits in the area left the two women alone, due to superstitions surrounding ill fortune and destitution falling upon anyone who violated the sanctuary of a provincial roadhouse.

Hua Yue grew up to be a musical prodigy and a lover of art. Visitors to the roadhouse have provided Qing Shan with all the necessary resources to raise Hua Yue with a proper education, even allowing Hua Yue to amass a collection of musical instruments — although most of these are of simple craftsmanship.

Niu2Tian1Shen2 (Niu Tian Shen, "Ox Lord of New Day's Toil"), the tutelary deity of the local region, receives his power from the sun and sows the fields. Several years ago, he was exploring his domain in human form when the gentle strains of Hua Yue's music mesmerized him. He started spending time at the provincial roadhouse regularly, always visiting in his human guise. Over time, he fell in love with the beautiful young Hua Yue.

Niu Tian Shen hid his true nature from Qing Shan and Hua Yue, leading them to believe he was just a traveling chronicler named Niu, but he secretly used his favor to help the roadhouse prosper. The gardens grew more bountiful, fewer vermin found their way onto the property, and the buildings seldom needed repair. The roadhouse was blessed with good fortune that had been unseen for generations. With each visit, Hua Yue found herself more enamored with the odd, massive man and eventually developed feelings of her own for him.

Niu Tian Shen's wife, *Mei3Lan2* (Mei Lan, "Beautiful Orchid"), a fairy, discovered that the man she loved and obsessed over was enamored with a mortal. Mei Lan decided in her rage that if her husband was going to love a human, that humans would be his undoing. Jealous and angry, she cast a spell into the seeds of a flower that she cast into the wind. The seeds' objective was to seek out a woman with greed, anger, and pain consuming her heart … and plant themselves within her. Of course, being "the doting, loving, and forgiving wife" that she is, she planned to use her *Shen2Xian1* (Taoist Immortal Fairy) powers to save her husband in the end, if he'd only see the error of his bullheaded ways.

The seed cast onto the wind by Mei Lan's found a woman named *Fei1Du2* (Fei Du, Flight and Study), Fei Du had been sold to her husband at a young age, badly treated, then discarded by him in favor of a mistress. While conventional religions taught Fei Du that she needed to work hard on herself and that she would be rewarded through lifetimes of reincarnation, she was impatient. Instead, she sought to become a *Shen2* (note: see the Monsters in Chinese Folklore Side box at the end of the chapter for an explanation of shen) through moral shortcuts and evil acts, not knowing — or not caring — that it would corrupt and twist her essence into something else.

> *Fei Du can also be written to mean "Fragrant Poison," but it would still be pronounced exactly the same in verbal communication. This is the name she adopted later in life when she becomes a cult leader.*

Fei Du studied legends and lore about those who gained power through supernatural means, scouring the lands and making deals in the dark. This ultimately led her to the discovery of a *soul gourd* hidden in the northern mountains, an item that once belonged to a vanquished immortal.

She experimented with the *soul gourd,* trapping people's souls and drinking them to extend her youth. She also discovered that great — but fleeting — power coursed through her veins after she drank.

Fei Du amassed followers and now presents herself as a savior to those who have suffered significant loss and spiraled into self-destructive patterns. She promises them the power to shape their own fates — possibly even to bring back what they have lost. She even shares small sips of her draught with the most devoted of her followers, empowering them to do her bidding.

Led to Fei Du by the seeds implanted in her, Mei Lan approached the cult leader and laid out a proposition. In exchange for Fei Du's and her cult's service, she would grant Fei Du's desire for everlasting power. As proof, Mei Lan provided Fei Du the means to capture and drink the souls of spirits in addition to those of humans. Intoxicated by this new power, Fei Du swore fealty to Mei Lan, not knowing she was merely a means to the fairy's ends.

Mei Lan convinced Fei Du to set her sights higher, on more powerful gods. She seeded the idea of taking the essence of Niu Tian Shen without ever specifically suggesting it. When Fei Du asked her patron for aid in capturing Niu Tian Shen, Mei Lan was more than happy to provide poison from a rare bird, the *Zhen4Niao3* (zhenniao, a daemon bird) to weaken the god. Armed with what she believed to be a foolproof plan, Fei Du sent a contingent of her most loyal followers to the provincial roadhouse to set her trap. This brings us to the present day.

The cultists arrived at the provincial roadhouse in the guise of weary merchants making their way to the Qixi Festival to sell their goods.

Note: Cultists are referred to using the masculine pronoun for ease of reading and writing. Given the coed nature of the cults, these unnamed cultists may be of either gender.

Armed with hidden weapons and poison, the cultists spent the night lying in wait to ambush Niu Tian Shen in the morning.

Niu Tian Shen, however, did not visit the next day, and so the cultists released the ox that pulled their cart and feigned that it had broken loose. They then pretended to search for the ox to no avail so they could spend a second night at the roadhouse.

Again, Niu Tian Shen did not appear the following morning either. So the cultists told Qing Shan that they would simply take turns pushing the cart until they could find a farm from which to purchase or borrow an ox. They went outside and started to push, but secretly used their blades to break the wagon wheel.

They then told Qing Shan that they'd been too hard on the cart, which caused it to catch in the road and break. The cultists spent yet a third night at the roadhouse.

The following morning, Niu Tian Shen arrived. Quickly, the cultists went into action. While the two caretakers of the roadhouse worked to put breakfast on the table for all the guests, one of the cultists sneaked to their cart and retrieved a bundle of blessed swords from a hidden compartment. Another cultist planted vials of poison around the tree in the courtyard.

Others loaded *zhenniao poison* darts into their sleeve dart guns and waited for the signal to strike.

Unfortunately, one of the cultists became nervous, and jumped into action before the signal. He attacked Qing Shan in the kitchen but she screamed, alerting everyone. She bolted for the dining room but her assailant caught her and thrust a knife through her back before she stepped through the open doorway. The overeager cultist slit her throat as a display of power before tossing her body aside to join the fight.

The attackers, however, had deeply underestimated the power of the god they were trifling with, for even in human form, Niu Tian Shen's mass and prowess were formidable. The combat quickly turned against the cultists. In a blur, the disguised Niu Tian Shen overpowered the cultists. Unable to complete their objective, the surviving cultists still managed to take Hua Yue hostage, whereupon they fled.

Niu Tian Shen intended to pursue, but he needed to gather his strength and heal his wounds, so he stumbled to the tree in the courtyard, one of this anchor points in the region, to borrow its lifeforce. When his hands touched the poisoned tree, he fell unconscious and lost his corporeal form.

Since then, Niu Tian Shen has been bound within the magically envenomed circle around the tree. Unable to flee elsewhere for healing, he has had two days to succumb to the poison and has devolved into madness.

Chapter Two:
The Provincial Roadhouse

The adventurers arrive on the third day after the attack on the roadhouse.

Start

Some of the characters may have information that precedes their arrival at the provincial roadhouse, involving the local animals and vegetation. Druids, rangers, and wilderness-oriented characters notice that the wildlife has quieted or become absent during the last two days of the party's travels. Last night, even the song of crickets did not accompany the characters when they camped under the sky.

Druids, herbalists, farmers, and plant-oriented characters may notice that the local flora has become especially dry and haggard over the past two days of travel, even for these summer months.

No die roll is required for the characters to notice the oddity of the area; it is automatically apparent to anyone attuned to nature. Once you have given out any of this information as needed, read or summarize the information below.

The Roadhouse

If the characters investigate the cart more closely, they can learn a few things with a successful Perception check:

DC 5:

- The crates and jars are partially filled with sand and dirt, and there's nothing of value. This should immediately strike the characters as odd. While the crates and jars are labelled to contain trade goods such as tools, linen, and lanterns, an inspection of their contents reveals they are partially filled with only regular sand and dirt.
- One of the cart's wheels is damaged. Beating the DC by 5 or more reveals that the wheel seems to have been intentionally broken using a bladed weapon. Coal dust is caught in the impact marks. A dirt-covered (quickly turning to mud) yoke for an ox is shoved into the back of the cart, the straps on it broken. Beating the DC by 5 or more reveals the straps were intentionally cut.

DC 10:

- One small box up by the driver's seat is filled with straw and wood shavings. Beating the DC by 5 or more reveals indentations for several small pouches that were once housed here. The pouches appeared to be porous in nature and left a small amount of herbal residue in the box.
- A light dusting of coal is under the protected tarp.

DC 15:

- A heavy blanket cascades out of a concealed compartment underneath the cart. This is where the cultists smuggled their swords. The swords were retrieved in a hurry; the compartment was left unpacked because the cultists assumed a sure victory and time to pack it away properly.

A-1. Foyer/Shrine

The stove shows is empty and has not been used in some time. This is common during summer months. The food offerings on the altar have spoiled and rotted.

Inside the House dish, the characters find the canine tooth of an animal along with several coins yet to be collected. The Spirit dish has a tightly rolled ball of pungent herbs covered with paper along with a small sum of *spirit money*. Wilderness-oriented characters can identify the tooth as being from a tiger. The pungent herbs match the residue found in the box by the driver's seat of the cart outside.

The characters should understand a few things at this point:

- It is customary for someone to greet travelers who visit roadhouses. The characters have not received a proper welcome.
- They are expected to pay respects to the local god by lighting incense, kneeling, and bowing several times before resting the incense in the holder. A few prayers are traditionally recited at this time.
- Travelers who are able to do so are also expected to leave a small donation in the dishes: standard money in the "House" dish and spirit money or herb effigy in the "Spirit" dish for the god. People make offerings and donations upon arriving, and some make additional offerings when they leave.

The characters find no evidence of the attack in this room, because the attackers came to the roadhouse under the guise of being weary travelers and did not strike until they were already. inside the compound.

Leigong grants characters who show proper reverence through prayer a single reroll during the course of the adventure. Characters can take the better result of the two rolls.

Map A: The Provincial Roadhouse

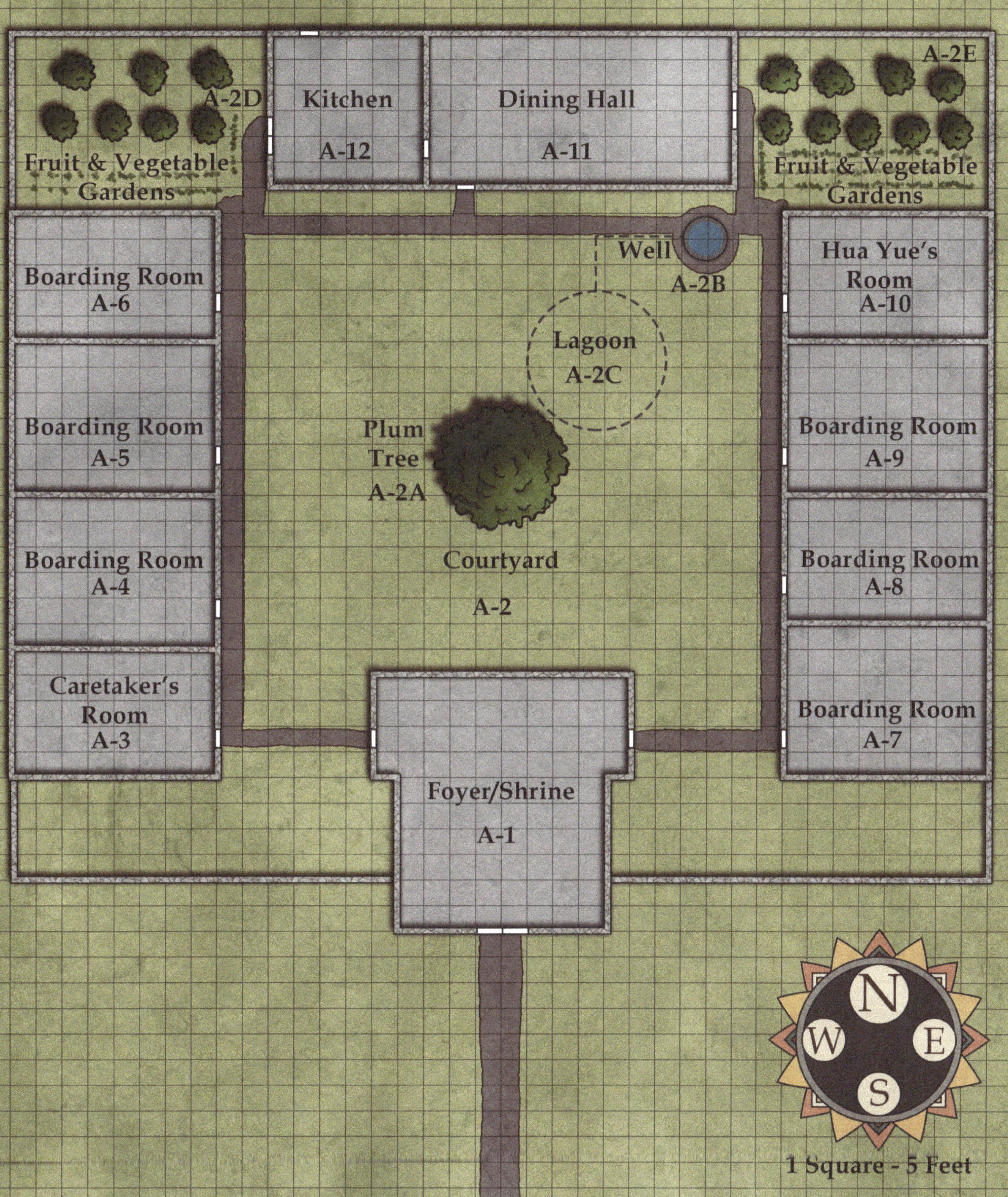

> You are looking out into a stone paved courtyard surrounded by the buildings of the roadhouse. The rain continues lashing down, and it is hot and muggy. Rain is unusual this time of year, and torrential rain like this is nearly unheard of. Your clothes immediately cling to you from a combination of your sweat and the rain blowing under eaves of the buildings.
>
> Several limestone benches are arranged around the courtyard along with one limestone table and five stools. What was once a magnificent plum tree with fruit still hanging from its branches stands in the center of the courtyard, but the entire tree is withered and rotting. There is a well in the far corner of the courtyard near a doorway.

Characters investigating the courtyard notice blood in the courtyard that the rain is quickly washing away on a successful DC 10 Perception check. Those who press their investigation despite the weather find traces of blood trails that can be tracked to two locations with a successful DC 20 Survival check. One blood trail leads to the dining hall (Area **A-11**). They can determine that the blood trail started in the kitchen and traveled into the courtyard. The other blood trail leads to the plum tree in the center of the courtyard but then disappears. They can determine that large humanoid footprints also end at the tree with a successful DC 18 Survival check.

If the characters stay sheltered under the awning and investigate other rooms in the compound first, the blood is washed away by the time they investigate the courtyard, increasing the DC of the Survival checks by 5 and of the Perception check by 20.

A-2A. The Plum Tree

Characters can find a large indentation where a human fell onto the earth beside the tree before disappearing with a successful DC 15 Perception check. Two large human handprints are burned into the tree trunk.

Characters who approach the plum tree hear snorting and clomping sounds when they are 15 feet out. If the characters continue to press and cross the 10-foot mark, **Niu Tian Shen (incorporeal form)** steps out from the tree, and attacks.

Every time Niu Tian Shen takes damage, the tree mirrors his wounds. Fruits wither and rot, and leaves change color and fall as the tree breaks apart.

Each time he's forced to fight, characters hear the deep rumbling bellows and snorts of a bull in pain. If the characters engage this manifestation but then retreat, the manifestation cannot pursue due to being caged inside the dirt-covered area around the tree. Niu Tian Shen slams against an invisible barrier before vanishing.

Niu Tian Shen (incorporeal form) CR 6
XP 2,400
hp 85 (Appendix C: New Monsters, "Niu Tian Shen [incorporeal form]")

Characters who attempt to communicate with Niu Tian Shen have to calm him, either through natural skill and talent or by playing music. Diplomacy is quite difficult here, requiring a successful DC 25 check to calm him, however, Perform skills calm him with a successful DC 20 check. Any characters skilled in musical instruments but don't have one with them may find something suitable in Hua Yue's room (area A-10). Hua Yue's xiao is exceptionally effective at calming him, reducing the DC on a Perform (wind instruments) check by 5.

If the characters are able to calm the manifestation, communication is still limited due to Niu Tian Shen's mental state — but they can get a few words such as "attacked," "poison," "monsters," and "love" between bellows, low growls, and snorts. Feel free to add garbled gibberish between the recognizable words.

There is a way to improve the god's condition, but it requires giving him a potion (see the "Yang's Potion" sidebox), which is not possible unless he manifests in corporeal form. Once the poison is removed from the tree, which will happen one way or another (see "After Nightfall"), Niu Tian Shen will materialize in corporeal form in the hills to the Northeast of the roadhouse at sunrise. If the characters have rescued the dragon Yang and talked with him, they may be in time to meet the god when he materializes in corporeal form, give him the potion, and bring him back to the dragon for additional help.

Freshly dug earth can be found about 10 feet out from the trunk. If **Niu Tian Shen (incorporeal form)** is calmed, defeated, or distracted by combat with other members of the party, characters investigating the upturned soil find five empty pouches planted equidistant in a ring around the tree.

The five empty pouches housed some sort of poison that disseminated into the earth around the tree. Each pouch contains remnants of one of the five elements planted in order around the tree: wood, fire, earth, metal, and water. The exterior of each pouch is marked with each element's hanzi written with smearing coal powder.

Characters can determine that these pouches are used to poison a shen's bond with their domain with a successful DC 25 Knowledge (religion) check. With time, they can also identify some of the components as fairy spit and a variety of herbs, and that the ingredients were combined with magic.

Characters familiar with poisons recognize the zhenniao feather barbs and spines packed into each pouch with a successful DC 20 Craft (alchemy) check..

A-2B. The Well

This appears to be a normal well. The taut rope hanging from it indicates a bucket at the bottom. A quick glance shows the bucket appears intact.

The Water Bucket

> The water ripples from the heavy rain splashing against it but the water looks fresh and clean. Bits of light glint against the bottom of the bucket from what appear to be large fish-scales about three inches in diameter.

Characters can easily discern that the scales are genuine silver and pearl with a successful DC 15 Appraise check. Characters who succeed at a DC 20 Knowledge (religion) check believe these scales came from a silver water dragon, the spirits and guardians of large bodies of water.

The well water tastes metallic and smells like rotting vegetation, but it is safe to drink — for now. The smell is so slight that a bucket of water must be pulled up for the characters to notice it. The waterline appears to be about 50 feet down the well.

Down the Well

Vegetation growing on the inner wall of the well provides good handholds and makes climbing down easier. Only one Medium-sized character can fit at a time into the diameter of the well. A character reaching midway down the well starts to hear faint echoes of speech (see the Mei Gen encounter below for the types of things that can be heard).

> As your feet touch the water, something slithers against one foot and reaches for your ankle. You scramble to ascend again but the rope-like vines growing against the well come to life and break apart. Boils of black ichor rise to the surface of each individual vine, making them look more like tentacles than plants. The ichor drips as they descend, attempting to wrap around you.

As soon as a character reaches the waterline, they are attacked by a **canker vine**.

Canker Vine   CR 8
XP 4,800
hp 150 (Appendix C: New Monsters, "Canker Vine")

Once the characters have defeated the canker vine, they will be able to see more of the space at the well bottom.

Following the cackle leads the characters to an underground lagoon.

A-2C. The Dragon's Lagoon

Mei Gen CR 8
XP 4,800
hp 92 (Appendix C: New Monsters, "Mogwai, Rot and Fecundity")

This mogui is *Mei2 Gen1* (Mei Gen, Rot Root). **Mei Gen** is clearly enraged at the interruption and exchanges haughty words with the characters before attacking to "dispose of the nuisance." If attacked, his eyes go black and green as lightning crackles from them. Listed below are some of the phrases he spouts at the characters; feel free to create your own based on these:

* "I didn't expect I'd get to have mortals for dessert so soon."

* "Leigong can't see so deep underground. What he can't see, he can't punish."

* "I'll feed your chi to my pets and make you into fertilizer."

If the characters defeat Mei Gen, the canker vines wrapped around the dragon *Yang2* (Yang, Ocean, Silver Coin) go limp and can easily be removed.

The dragon **Yang** is grateful for being rescued but rolls his eyes and feigns boredom if the characters become impatient trying to get his attention. Yang finally addresses the characters after a few laps. Yang is currently regenerating in the water. He is a little bit lazy but enjoys riddles and proverbs. In his mind, he always has time and many beings are just too impatient.

Yang   CR 8
XP 4,800
hp 85 (Pathfinder Roleplaying Game Bestiary 3, "Sea Dragon, Young")

Yang thanks the characters and introduces himself. The characters may have varying degrees of information depending upon how much of the roadhouse they have explored. After any initial pleasantries, the conversation will most likely begin with the quote from the text box below.

This is likely to cause the characters to ask questions about "the ox," and the conversation can proceed — approximately — along these lines. Depending on the questions the characters ask, not all of these points may get raised.

* The ox was attacked a couple of days ago.
* "The ox lives above but he also lives in the hills to the northeast. He comes to the place above often. He visits me sometimes, but he always wants something. It's always boring work that I don't want to do."
* Characters should get the impression that Yang finds Niu Tian Shen annoying and bothersome. Yang rolls his eyes, sighs, and shrugs a lot.
* "Ox comes in human form to visit the mortal girl above. She intoxicates him with her music, and he's enamored." Yang clearly disapproves of Niu Tian Shen's infatuation with the mortal.
* He mentions that the ox believes it is true love. If the characters press Yang about Niu Tian Shen's romantic life, the dragon may mention that the ox is rumored to be married to a fairy that lives high in the northwest mountains. Ox never goes into the mountains though.

Whenever it seems appropriate, Yang will make his request to the characters, roughly as follows:

If the characters ask what Yang means about "falling victim", he'll explain. "The ox is dying, and with him, the land. I have heard stories of deserts in distant lands where gods fought and died, but I have never seen it with my own eyes. I do not wish to see it."

If the characters agree to help, Yang pulls a small pearl vial from the sleeve of his robe. "Once you calm him, make him drink this. It suppresses the madness, temporarily, and should allow you to communicate with him."

If the characters demand payment, they obviously offend Yang. He reluctantly offers a handful of molted scales worth 2,000 gp but expects the characters to realize the error of their ways and decline. If any characters accept this payment, they are marked with his disfavor.

If the characters don't ask for payment, Yang remembers the characters and favors them in the future.

He encourages them to bring the ox to him because he believes he can diagnose the poison. It is possible he can design a cure if the characters help procure the rare ingredients.

Yang tells the characters that they should seek the ox out in the morning light on the pastures in the hills to the northeast. Touched by the rays of the sun, he should take the corporeal form of an oversized ox.

Yang provides the characters with very clear landmarks and says it should be a two to three hour walk for a human. It is important that they make it before high sun. He also warns the characters that the ox will not be in his right mind so they need to subdue or calm him.

If asked about music, Yang laughs and says, "Who is to say the ox wasn't mad before the poison? He did cut off his own horn and fashion it into a xiao (a vertical end-blown flute) for his mortal love. I'd never cut off my beautiful mane for anyone." He punctuates his statement by running a hand through his hair, pulling it forward over his shoulder. He then recites a proverb, "Those who hear not the music, think the dancers mad," and shrugs.

If presented with the coal pendants or the coal-covered sword with gelsemium on it (found in area A-7), Yang pulls away, muttering a prayer, "Leigong protect me from such a fate." He is clearly scared and speaks in a hushed whisper about rumors of a dark cult that seeks power by taking the souls of daemons such as himself and the ox. He will also, if asked, explain who Leigong is (see the adventure start for details — Leigong is the disguised thunder god the characters met at the beginning of the adventure).

He can also give them the information that gelsemium is extremely poisonous to humans and many animals but has no effect on daemons, so it couldn't be what poisoned the ox.

"Several water sprites bring me fresh water from the mountains, and they tell me about the Tan4shi4 (Tanshi, coal addicts) working their waters, hiding underneath the mountains. The sprites say their leader is called Fragrant Poison. I think they are a dark cult seeking power and ascension through unnatural means."

"The water sprites say that the dark cult has caught a few of their number in the past but most of them are too fast and able to hide from the cultists."

A-2D. AND A-2E. FRUIT AND VEGETABLE GARDENS

These two areas cannot be seen or accessed from the main courtyard.

However, one peach tree in area A-2D is worth noting:

These peaches are a gift to the characters from Leigong to reward and assist them. When eaten, they heal 9 hit points and allow characters an additional save with a +2 divine bonus against any diseases or poisons affecting them.

The tree has 4 peaches.

A-3. CARETAKER'S ROOM

This is Qing Shan's room. Characters searching the room may find a small hiding space dug into the dirt under some floorboards by the bed. An old, dust-covered box rests inside and contains a wrapped martial arts manual titled *Day of the Seven Cranes*.

A-4. THROUGH A-9. BOARDING ROOMS

These boarding rooms for travelers are all uniform and relatively sparse. The furniture is functional and serviceable but not new or expensive. Each room includes a nook-style bed, a table and two chairs, a tea set on the table, a ceramic latrine basin, and a mirror-less vanity with a large bowl and a pitcher.

Characters searching these rooms find a couple of travel satchels with basic travel necessities such as water gourds. A little coal dust is found on all of the satchels.

In the first two rooms the characters choose to investigate, they hear the chittering of rats nearby but won't find any to engage. The third room the characters investigate contains 1d4 **rat swarms**.

Rat Swarm (4)   CR 2
XP 600
hp 16 (Pathfinder Roleplaying Game Bestiary, "Rat Swarm")

In Area A-7, the characters find a sword hidden in a travel-bedroll one of the cultists left behind with a successful DC 20 Perception check. The weapon is in a poorly fitting sheath. Gelsemium flowers are engraved along the metal blade, which is also covered in coal dust. Recognizing the flowers requires a successful DC 10 Knowledge (nature) check. Characters may know that the coal dust is a trick assassins and some cults use so that their weapons don't catch the light with a successful DC 15 Stealth check. Characters may recall another name for these flowers with a successful DC 15 Knowledge (nature) check: heartbreaker's grass. It is known to be an exceptionally poisonous yellow flowering plant.

A-10. Hua Yue's Room

Entering this room, you can see that someone took great care to decorate and maintain it. Each wall is covered with a white silk screen painted with mountains and meadows, and overlaid with poems written vertically from right to left. The calligraphy here matches that on the banners in the shrine.

A bed is on the far end of the room. The frame is built into the ceiling, and panels come around the front. Several layers of curtains hang down just past the mattress. To the left of the door, a low table functions as a desk and has embroidery, painting, and sewing projects cluttering its surface. This room includes the washbasin and latrine from the other rooms, but the vanity here has a mirror, unlike the others.

Scattered all around the room are musical instruments, mostly of simple craftsmanship and not much in the way of decoration.

Two instruments stand out from the rest. A guqin, a seven-stringed zither, is decorated with inlaid coral shaped into a winged serpent. The other is a xiao, a vertical end-blown flute usually made of bamboo. This is *Hua Yue's xiao*, which has a scene of a woman dancing her way to the mountains skillfully carved into the material. Closer inspection reveals that it is made from an animal horn and not the expected bamboo. The xiao detects as magical.

Hue Yue's xiao is made from the horn of Niu Tian Shen, who has a close spiritual connection to it. Given the strength of the connection and the pure nature of the xiao, Niu Tian Shen is able to burst the bonds holding him near the tree so he can defend the xiao from theft.

If characters remove the xiao from Hua Yue's room without playing it, **Niu Tian Shen (incorporeal form)** forms outside the room and attacks, trying to knock them back into the room (if the characters haven't already defeated him in the courtyard). The manifestation continues to attack the bearer of the xiao, gaining the effects of *rage* against the target of his ire.

The characters may manage to calm Niu Tian Shen by their diplomatic skills or by playing the xiao: see Area **A2-A**.

Niu Tian Shen (incorporeal form) CR 6
XP 2,400
hp 85 (Appendix C: New Monsters, "Niu Tian Shen [incorporeal form]")

Searching the room uncovers a journal Hua Yue kept in her desk (or under her pillow). Flipping through it, characters find a few passages of interest:

Journal Excerpt A

I couldn't sleep again last night so I sneaked out under the moonlight and followed the stars. It was morning by the time I stopped on the hills in a beautiful pasture with spring flowers sprouting between the wild grass. From it, I can look down into the distance and see where I came from. The roadhouse is so small that I couldn't even pick it out in the distance.

I fell asleep in the grass. When I woke, a huge ox was standing still and staring at me. I was terrified at first, even screamed, but somehow the ox looked concerned for me and snorted several times.

When he didn't make a move toward me, I picked a handful of grass and offered it to him, then played music while he grazed beside me. I could have sworn he was dancing.

Journal Excerpt B

Mother says Master Niu sent word he'd be visiting tomorrow morning. I can't wait to play the xiao for him. It was such an extravagant gift; I can't imagine how much it cost. I wrote several songs for Master Niu. I'm so nervous. I hope he likes them.

Journal Excerpt C

I'm beginning to understand why mountains are the gateway to heaven. I brought a picnic to the hill today, my personal heaven. I made sure to bring some fruit in case the ox was there.

Oh, the horror! Poor ox lost a horn! I wish he could tell me what happened. I worry it hurts him. He ate the fruit from my hand and licked the juice off my arm. At least he's in good spirits despite missing one of his horns now.

Several other entries reference regular visits to the hill along with sketches of the area and the view from the hilltop. The characters can use these sketches and some basic knowledge to map their way to the location if they think of it.

In the entries, Hua Yue often mentions encountering Master Niu on the hilltop on a regular basis. She tends to detail those encounters with extreme care. Though she never comes out and writes it in her journal, there's a strong implication that Hua Yue has a significant crush on Master Niu.

Several other entries mention occasional encounters with the ox on the hilltop and the rapport the two built through music. She even comments on the absolute hilarity of watching the ox dance.

A-11. Dining Hall

Stepping into the dining hall, you come upon a horrific scene and the smell of death. What was once a rectangular wooden table and a dozen chairs is now a mess of broken and splintered wood. Three men and a woman are dead in this room, a couple of them draped over the broken furniture. Blades and blowguns lie just out of their grasps.

The corpses have begun to sprout a variety of fungi, mushrooms, and molds, with a large pool of blood producing a rainbow-colored growth. Their faces are obscured or decayed beyond recognition.

The door to the kitchen is closed, but you pick up the distinct scent of fresh steamed baozi, rice, and vegetables in the air mixing with the smell of rot and decay in the dining hall. Sounds of metal on metal can be heard from the kitchen.

A half dozen coal-dusted swords, two coal-dusted daggers, and two blowguns can be found scattered around the room. A number of the surviving attackers dropped their weapons as they fled with their hostage.

Characters who succeed at a DC 15 Stealth check note that covering a blade with coal or soot is a way assassins avoid having the blades reflect light and giving away their position.

The bodies of the men and women are dressed alike, with each wearing gray linen robes with white robes lining them. The only sign of wealth in their clothes is a red silk sash around their waist, marking them as poor merchants. All their clothes and the weapons found around this room have coal dust on them.

Investigating the bodies reveals that each one wears a pendant carved of chunks of coal. A seal is stamped onto each of them in red. The seals read "Duan Chan Cao" ("Heartbreaker Grass"). The bottom of each of these chunks of coal has been fashioned into a chop (a stamp most often used among the wealthy as their signature). Each chop has a different inscription.

Further investigation reveals that each body has several harnesses and scabbards designed to conceal a small weapon. One of them is also carrying a regional map with the roadhouse specifically marked on it (see **Cultist's Map**).

Characters investigating the corpses have a 1-in-3 chance of discovering and being attacked by **rot grubs**!

Rot Grub Swarm CR 7
XP 3,200
hp 85 (Pathfinder Roleplaying Bestiary 3, "Rot Grub Swarm")

A-12. Kitchen

The kitchen is bustling with activity. A middle-aged woman dressed in a floral robe soaked in blood stands over the stove with a wok in one hand and a metal spatula in the other. A stacked bamboo steamer nestled in another wok is over another section of the stove.

A closer look reveals that the woman's throat has been slit, her neck wound providing a gruesome second smile where the blood dried. Her disheveled hair is pulled up into a bun, but loose strands are matted with dried blood, gluing bits of it to her face and neck. A dagger runs through her from back to sternum.

This is **Qing Shan**, who is now a chi thief mogwai. She can talk with the characters but cannot provide any useful information because her attackers slit her throat so "she can tell no secrets" after they killed her. Her throat wasn't slit deep enough to render her mute, however. Characters who succeed at a DC 20 Knowledge (planes or religion) check will perceive that the slit throat acts as a curse on her.

> The woman seems startled by your presence but turns to greet you. She attempts to smile, but the dead flesh on her face causes her face to contort strangely.
>
> "Hello, hello! I trust my daughter has you settling in? Our humble roadhouse is getting quite full but I'm sure we'll find space to keep you all comfortable during your short stay! Go have a seat in the hall. Dinner's almost ready, and I made some baozi for you to travel with in the morning!"

Qing Shan is able to answer basic questions but does not remember the attack or details of her death:

- "I'm Qing Shan. My daughter and I keep this place running and travelers fed."
- "My daughter? Her name is Hua Yue. She's the one who greeted you when you arrived."
- "Three days ago, nine merchants arrived and suffered bad luck day after day so they stayed far longer than they expected. They weren't very sociable, so I mostly just let them be except for meals. (Her timing is off; it's actually been five days, because she stopped being able to track time when she died.)
- If the characters push Qing Shan to remember what happened, she'll explain things away with statements such as, "Oh, Hua Yue's probably run off to her hills again." Get creative if pressed for more.
- If the characters manage to find a way to force Qing Shan to confront her condition, she will turn on the characters and attack. She will lose what memories she does have until her next return.

Qing Shan   **CR 4**
XP 1,200
hp 37 (Appendix C: New Monsters, "Mogwai, Chi Thief")

Speak with dead will not produce more information without first casting *remove curse* on her. Qing Shan's timing will be accurate if questioned under a *speak with dead* spell, and she gives accurate accounts of the information she knows.

Qing shan is a mogui but of a different subtype than Mei Gen. If the characters fight and defeat her, she rises again at moonrise and returns to maintaining the grounds by sweeping the courtyard, watering the dying plants, picking dying plants to cook, and cooking in the kitchen. Each time she rises in this way, she is a more diminished version of her human self and becomes more easily angered and aggressive.

If the characters chop her into tiny bits, char her to dust, or make Qing Shan mush, she comes back without a body and is far more dangerous. Characters who make a successful DC 20 Knowledge (religion) may know that a mogui without a body is prone to possessing those who do.

The only way to truly lay Qing Shan to rest is to have a suitable monk, cleric, priest, or family member perform a transition ceremony that includes the burning of spirit money and special incense. A cleric character can perform the ceremony.

A-13. Cellar

This cellar is little more than a five-foot-deep pit filled with varying sizes of ceramic jars. Some are used to store dry goods while others store fermenting foods. There's just enough space for one Medium-sized creature to enter the pit and get to the stored foodstuffs.

Unfortunately, the accelerated corruption and rot which affects the roadhouse has already spread into this storage. About 50% of the containers of dried rice, seeds, nuts, and fruits are still edible, and 30% of the fermented products including dry and wet brined pickled peppers and various vegetables are still edible.

Characters find a *+1 silver weapon* (fitting what someone in the group would use), 6 *potions of cure light wounds* nestled in a box covered with sawdust and straw, and a spirit stone (a *stone of good luck [luckstone]*) stashed behind several fermentation jars on a shelf built into the wall. All of it looks rather old, untouched for quite some time.

The spirit stone is a piece of white jade shaped like a gourd with a red string and ornate knotting tied around it.

After Nightfall (Unfinished Business)

The rain stops around midnight but rumblings of thunder and occasional flashes of lightning ring in the distance well into midmorning.

Late in the night, *if the characters haven't already pulled the poison satchels from around the tree in the courtyard*, the rotting bark and bugs peel off the tree and shape into hands crawling around the courtyard searching for something. There are 4 fetid hand swarms meandering around.

Fetid Hands Swarm (4)   **CR 1**
XP 400
hp 9 (Appendix C: New Monsters, "Fetid Hands Swarm")

Some of these hands start digging at the dirt around the tree, tearing up roots and revealing the five buried pouches. Others crawl around the courtyard and possibly even make their way into rooms where the characters are spending the night. These hands crawl across the dark floor or drop out of the rafters. Characters are far more likely to smell them before they see them.

After dealing with these hands, the characters find the poison pouches unearthed and displaced. Niu Tian Shen has been released and appears later in the hills.

An hour or two before dawn, if the characters haven't already explored the lagoon, they hear the sound of painful whimpers echoing up to the courtyard from the well.

Yang is far weaker if rescued at this time. He provides the same information as before but is far less playful about it, curling up in a ball on the islet in human form and on the edge of sleep during the entire conversation.

The Northeast Hills are approximately a two to three hour walk. Mention that the characters still hear the rumbling of distant thunderclaps during their journey despite it no longer raining or a cloud even appearing in the sky.

Niu Tian Shan appears on the hilltop at sunrise, and shortly thereafter a group of cultists arrive and attack him. Depending on when the characters arrive, they may have a chance to subdue and question the maddened god before the cultists come onto the scene.

> Even diminished by the poison you now know is festering in the land and its god, the hills northeast of the roadhouse are a place of beauty. Hiking up the hillsides, the grass grows taller, and you weave through copses of bamboo trees. What was likely green and verdant just a week ago now shows signs of drying and wilting. Leaves on some of the trees are wilting.
>
> White, yellow, and red wildflowers dot the landscape, many missing some or half their petals. They reach for the sun along with the tall grass that stretches more than three feet high by the time you reach the hilltop.

Regardless of how things develop, the characters observe that whenever Niu Tian Shen exerts himself, the plants around him begin to die.

ARRIVING BEFORE SUNRISE

Characters who arrive before dawn are able to set up whatever procedures and precautions they would like while waiting for the ox's arrival. If they are looking for cover, the slope of the hillside and the tall grass are both options.

> As the sun crests over the mountains, you watch the hilltop for any signs of the ox. Sunlight catches on something you can't see, and it flares bright, momentarily blinding you. When your senses return, a massive ox with one horn and gashes in it shoulder and sides stands before you. It snorts, smelling the air, and clomps its hooves against the ground several times before backing away from your position and collapsing into the tall grass.

Niu Tian Shen　　CR 8
XP 4,800
hp 101 (Appendix C: New Monsters, "Niu Tian Shen")

If Niu Tian Shen is calmed or subdued, the characters can use the draught Yang gave them to temporarily suppress his madness. Characters could also cast *neutralize poison* on Niu Tian Shen to make the draught's effect permanent and remove the poison, but it requires far more powerful magic than the characters have available to actually restore Niu Tian Shen to health.

MEMORIES OF NIU TIAN SHEN

At first, Niu Tian Shen is quite disoriented. Characters may need to pose questions, prompt him and fill in information they have gathered. Memories return in bits and pieces, but a complete picture can be formed by interacting with the characters.

Niu Tian Shen was looking in on his friends Matron Shan and her daughter, Hua Yue. Time hasn't been passing logically for him since he was poisoned, but with the characters filling in information, he guesses it happened four or five mornings ago.

He remembers the provincial roadhouse being filled with more guests than he'd seen in years, but not liking the smell of coal and filth that clung to the merchants gathering in the dining hall for breakfast. Matron Shan made porridge and fried dough with sweetened hot soy milk to drink. Thoughts of Matron Shan's food quickly distracts Niu Tian Shen. He rambles on about the various dishes she cooks and how they are all of the best quality.

He remembers Matron Shan screaming. He ran inside to help and was attacked. A moment later, a man emerged from the kitchen with Matron Shan's limp form shielding him. The assassin slit her throat before casting her aside.

Thinking back to before the fight, Niu Tian Shen recalls that one of the attackers might have slipped out to the cart parked outside and fetched larger bladed weapons. He saw a man bring a large, blanket-wrapped bundle in on his back but didn't think anything of it at the time.

After the fight, Niu Tian Shen recalls that he pulled himself to the plum tree, an anchor of his power. He hoped to re-energize himself with the divine essence imbued in the tree. However, when he pulled upon the energy within the tree, he discovered it was poisoned and corrupt. He can't remember or make sense of anything after that.

Everything after that is a haze, but he does remember someone calling out about orders "not to kill the girl." He had a panic attack when he realized he'd lost track of Hua Yue.

Unless he's captured and imprisoned by appropriate means, he remains anchored to this hilltop until he either heals or dies. Each morning, he returns to the hilltop as the sun crests the mountains.

He has other anchors across the region but this is the center of his power and where he is tied to most strongly. The nearest other tether is the poisoned plum tree in the roadhouse courtyard. But he is unable to return there due to the corruption ritual the cultists performed.

Unless the characters leave very shortly, they will be present when the cultists attack.

Cultist's Map

Arriving After Sunrise

Characters who arrive on the hilltop before high sun but after sunrise see cultists attacking Niu Tian Shen, who is currently manifested as an unusually large ox.

The characters ascend the opposite side of the hill from the cultists, so they are unlikely to notice the cultists before the attack.

Niu Tian Shen will have little to no effect on a battle between the characters and the cultists, given his condition. The characters will have to defeat the cultists without any measurable help from the god. The battle involves **1 cultist lieutenant, 1 cultist assassin, 1 cultist magic user, and 2 cultist monks.**

Cultist Assassin CR 5
XP 1,600
hp 45 (Pathfinder Roleplaying Game GameMastery Guide, "Tomb Raider")

Cultist Lieutenant   CR 5
XP 1,600
hp 48 (Pathfinder Campaign Setting Inner Sea NPC Codex, "Silent Enforcer")

Cultist Magic User   CR 5
XP 1,600
hp 33 (Pathfinder Roleplaying Game GameMastery Guide, "Battle Mage")

Cultist Monk (2) CR 4
XP 1,200
hp 31 (Pathfinder Roleplaying Game NPC Codex, "Cruel Devotee")

The cultists have a map showing a section of the region that includes the provincial roadhouse in the lower right corner and Mei Zhen on the upper left corner.

Questioning any captured cultists yields some information:

- The cultist is a devotee of Fragrant Poison, their great leader. She is so powerful that the goddess Mei Lan sought her out and promised her people a great future.
- The cultist doesn't fear death because they believe Mei Lan will reward them for their sacrifice.
- Becoming a cultist involved a ritual separation from the cultist's former life. They gave up property, name, and personal identity as a sacrifice to Fragrant Poison in preparation for true enlightenment. Every cultist is required to make this sacrifice.

Characters who develop a rapport with the cultist might make headway in reversing the brainwashing. Characters may be able to play on the cultist's previous identity to provide the fanatic some clarity and perspective with a successful DC 20 Diplomacy check. Doing so yields some better information:

- Their temple is located near Meizhen to the southeast. It is hidden deep below an abandoned mine.
- Fragrant Poison has a powerful magic item, but the cultist doesn't know the nature of its power.
- Characters need a key to enter the "great temple."
- Fragrant Poison and her followers used to operate out of abandoned houses in the recesses of the southern mountains until their new patron goddess moved them to the "great temple" a few months ago.
- Their new patron goddess created a magical doorway that the cultists use to enter the "great temple." The cultists wear chops around their necks; every supplicant must wear one to enter.
- This group was sent out when the provincial roadhouse attack failed.

Niu Tian Shen is scared, and attacks at the slightest provocation, but he can be calmed by playing the xiao or by diplomatic skill. Characters who examine him after the battle with the cultists find barbs and broken shafts from *zhenniao* bird feathers in several of the wounds. Extracting them without doing more damage requires a successful DC 15 Heal check. Talking with the god after the cultist attack, provided he is calmed and given Yang's potion, yields the same information as if the characters had arrived before sunrise.

Returning to Yang

With the information the characters learn on the hill, they may choose to return to Yang with or without Niu Tian Shen, possibly hoping they can get him some help before the next morning light.

Read or summarize the following if the characters return to Yang during the day:

Read or summarize the following if the characters return to Yang during the night:

Yang   CR 8
XP 4,800
hp 85 (Pathfinder Roleplaying Game Bestiary 3, "Sea Dragon, Young")

If the characters didn't bring Niu Tian Shen with them, Yang is initially disappointed. He listens to what the characters learned, offering minimal feedback.

If the characters brought Niu Tian Shen with them, Yang pulls him deeper into the lagoon and attempts to heal him with the water and his powers. He encourages the characters to share what they've learned while he works.

Either way, Yang shakes his head in frustration when the characters finish catching him up on their progress and discoveries.

Yang emphasizes that it has to be something born of the beast such as a tooth, claw, feather, tuft of fur, or anything else that is suitable for dipping into ink. One possibility would be the tiger tooth the characters may have discovered in the foyer/shrine (area **A-1**).

Characters can also offer items from their equipment that they feel fit this description if they give a good enough reason.

Adjust the following boxed text with the item and corresponding animal:

After due consideration and conversation with the characters, Yang will help the characters arrive at the conclusion that Niu Tian Shen's horn must be restored. Gifts are sacred and the horn was gifted to Hua Yue so she must return it sincerely and freely. This is why Mei Lan gave the cultists specific instructions not to harm the girl. She needs Hua Yue alive and well to control her husband when the horn is returned to him as part of her plan.

If the characters have obtained the cultists' map and mention it to Yang, he will ask to see it. When he has looked at it, he will point out it is a map of the local region.

Chapter Four: Mei Zhen

(Coal Town)

By now, the characters should have enough information to realize that the coal mine near Mei Zhen is in some way associated with the goings-on at the roadhouse, and they will presumably head in that direction.

The characters must travel up a series of small roads and travel-beaten paths born that takes them northwest to Mei Zhen. The journey takes approximately two days.

Along the way, the characters cross paths with miners, tradesman, and tourists during the latter half of the journey.

The characters continue hearing distant thunderclaps during their trip but these are relatively rare.

Gathering Information in Coal Town

When the characters arrive in Mei Zhen, the town's modest Qixi festivities are in full swing. They arrive on the third or fourth day of the seventh month depending on their travel plans. While not a metropolitan city like Weifeng, Mei Zhen receives its share of tourists due to its mistaken namesakes of "Plum Flower Town".

The locals aren't as jovial or festive as they are most years, given the recent troubles with people going missing in the mines, talks of people being cursed, and supplies going missing. They are generally putting on a brave face.

Slow rhythmic thunder beats through Mei Zhen when you arrive, although it is not raining. Street stalls filled with food and wares line the way into the town square where the statue of a tree has been molded out of coal. Paper plum flowers are affixed to the branches in abundance.

The general flow of traffic leads the characters toward the town's square where an acrobatic troupe is performing around the tree. A man with a set of drums sits at the base of the tree, and the characters realize that the sound of thunder they have been hearing is actually the beating of this drum.

Besides the slow rhythmic thunder of the red drum, the man's fingers are also tapping a quick and light rain sound. His long black hair has shocks of white playing in it, something you hadn't noticed during your first encounter. His booming laughter mixes into the music being played like a harmony synchronized with the melody. You quickly recognize the man's red winged robes as the good samaritan who told you about the washed-out road a few days earlier.

Leigong

Once again, the old man is Leigong the Thunder God. Leigong introduces himself as Lei Lao Ye (Old Man Lei). Religious characters may recognize some odd similarities between Lei Lao Ye and stories of Leigong that they may have heard with a successful DC 15 Knowledge (religion) check. Allow them to see resemblances but no outward assumptions.

He mentions that he recognizes the group but claims he can't quite place where they met before. When reminded, he laughs, "Oh, yes. My old addled mind. Come, you must be hungry. I know a little place with the best dumplings in the region!"

Lei Lao Ye is a larger-than-life drummer with a bit of a belly. When walking down the street with the characters, he alternates between drumming on his belly and the drum strapped to his side. He's a man of high spirits, and his presence easily fills up the room. He buys a round of drinks and meals for everyone in the establishment.

"So, did you get lost and turned around? Thought you all were heading to Weifeng? I hear the festivities there are pretty epic." If the characters share the reason for their visit to Mei Zhen, Lei Lao Ye mentions that there have been some rumors of troubles in the short time he's been in town but it's all very hush-hush.

He mentions that all the inns are full, but he's staying with some performers. They have a spare room the characters can share if they intend to spend the night.

Asking Around

The characters are able to move about town speaking with locals to learn some information. In general, people are welcoming despite being a little scared. They try to push characters into buying merchandise and items for the festival. Characters must build a little rapport with the townsfolk to loosen their tongues.

Goods for Sale

Items being sold for the Qixi festival include carvings of exotic flowers, animals, and unusual birds. These are usually carved into melon skins but some dealers also offer carvings on wood and coal. A variety of teas, fruits, nuts, and melon seeds are being sold as offerings to the weaver fairy. Bundles of wildflowers are woven for hanging on oxen effigies, and fried pastries flavored for every fruit and flower can be found for indulging on. Qixi is also one of several holidays when skilled craftsmen travel to cities to peddle their services and wares. All the food will be void of animal products.

Talking to Miners

A couple of miners are gathered in tea and entertainment houses share stories for proper libations, vegetarian food, and good company.

The mining process involves digging a pit in the ground, setting up a pulley system up top much like a water well and sending miners down with bamboo ladders to harvest while they tunnel.

In General

Most of the people in the area laugh off any talk of cultists, saying things like, "Children's stories to make them behave," or "If coal-loving cultists exist, maybe I should join them. They have magical ways of mining that won't hurt my back?" or "Can the cultists regrow the leg I lost in a mining accident?"

The Elderly Miner

One elderly, superstitious miner tells the characters about a pit they abandoned after breaking through to the third level of Diyu (Hell), the Hell of Boiling Sands. It is a place where you burn in an ocean of hot sand and dirt. The sand itself comes alive to drag you into the smoldering heat and causes you to suffer eternal suffocation. He's very insistent that a number of young miners were pulled deep into the boiling sands by living sand. He tried to stop the search party but his warnings fell on deaf ears. When a handful of the search party returned, they were "as white as the dead." One went mad; the others packed up and left. The one who went mad is known as the "Wrapped Man."

Either the Elderly Miner or the Wrapped Man can give the characters directions to the Coal Pit entrance to Nuwa's Fallen Palace.

The Wrapped Man

Characters can easily track down the maddened man, who is known around town as Lao Bao (The Wrapped Man). He's is a panhandler who surrounds himself with red lanterns. He wraps his hat, shoes, and walking stick in strips of paper with calligraphy painted across it. The characters can immediately tell that those letters are attempts at *Fu2lu4* (Fulu, Taoist magic script).

Characters who understand the arcane or divine note that the fulu was not done properly and has no magical effect.

Lao Bao rants and rambles at anyone who will listen, "The dark ones, they came for my soul. They'll come for your soul." Characters who try to redirect or interrupt anger him. "You don't understand! They come in the night! They take us to feed their dark gods! Blood in the alleys. … Families from their beds …"

The Frightened Miner

Over drinks, a miner brings up that before they abandoned the cursed mine, he saw something strange one night. He left his tent to relieve himself and spotted a group of people all dressed in the same dark clothes. He leans in conspiratorially and adds, "It was a bright moon that night, not quite full but I saw they all had big hanzi drawn across their faces." He watched them approach a cliff where the earth folded in on itself to create a "V" in the wall. One by one, they disappeared into it. He peed his pants and took off back to town, leaving all his mining gear in the camp. "I ran all night …"

The Frightened Miner can give the characters directions that take them to the Cultists' Entrance to Nuwa's Fallen Palace. He will not accompany them to the place, however.

Talking to Townsfolk

The characters detect magical and fake fulu hanging from doorways and windows all around town. Inquiring about them with the owners of the homes and businesses reveals that the town has been suffering some bad luck in recent months.

People started going missing in the night three or four month ago. One at a time, a few days apart, and with no predictable pattern. It hasn't happened in about three weeks though.

Supplies also started to go missing regularly about four months ago. Expected shipments sometimes never arrived. There are no reports of banditry causing it, but people are worried there might be a food supply shortage if this continues.

Tools have been breaking unexpectedly, which causes some to whisper of the town being cursed.

Others instead argue that "Old Man *Fu2* (Fu, "charm/talisman") never cared for his tools," or "*Guan1Po2* (Guan Po, "Matron Mountain Pass/To Close or Shut") bought the shovel from *Bai2Zhu2* (Baizhu, "White Candle"). Everyone knows he uses cheap materials and cuts corners. Of course it broke!"

Characters inquiring where people get the legitimate fulu learn that a holy man who lives in a small shrine to Leigong just outside town created them. People simply call him *Lao3Ye2* (Lao Ye, "Old Grandpa"); no one knows his real name.

Lao Ye

Lao Ye is a grizzled old retired monster hunter with scars across his face and body to prove it. He's willing to make each character up to two fulu if they make donations to the shrine worth at least 100 gp per character.

It takes roughly one hour to prepare himself to craft the fulu and an additional hour per fulu he makes.

Each fulu he makes wards the character from one save during their encounter with Fei Du. This includes the poison tea. The characters may not even realize they were the targets of the save because the wards redirect the effects to the scroll.

The Situation

Cultists are hiding among the civilians in Mei Zhen. They are participating in the festivities, selling goods as street vendors, and maybe even working as servers. Characters asking questions likely get their attention.

The cultists pay a street urchin to keep an eye on the characters. If the characters catch the street rat, he knows nothing about a cult and says he was just paid to keep an eye on the nosy tourists and report to a vendor selling coal-based artwork. Characters can pay the child more to point out the vendor who hired them. If the characters want to confront the coal-art vendor, remind them that they are in the midst of the Qixi festivities. There's a good crowd celebrating.

If they approach, the vendor's assistant intercepts the characters, asking if she can help them. The vendor uses this distraction to slip into the crowd and head toward a nearby residence. He's not trying to be particularly stealthy because he actually wants the characters to follow him. A large group of cultists is waiting to spring an ambush.

If the characters follow the vendor into the courtyard, **24 cultists** flood out of the buildings all around them while **12 dart blowers** pop up on the rooftops. The building in front of them is two stories tall while the ones on the left and right are only a single story.

If stealth or alternative methods are used to follow the "bait," the characters may be able to gather enough information to adjust the odds in their favor.

This fight is built to take place at multiple heights and is set up in an area where *fireballs* and other major area-of-effect spells should hit only one-third to half of the enemies at a time.

Cultist Assassin CR 5
XP 1,600
hp 45 (Pathfinder Roleplaying Game GameMastery Guide, "Tomb Raider")

Cultist Dart Blower (12)   CR 4
XP 1,200
hp 37 (Pathfinder Campaign Setting Inner Sea NPC Codex, "Sodden Scavenger")

Cultist Lieutenant (2)   CR 5
XP 1,600
hp 48 (Pathfinder Campaign Setting Inner Sea NPC Codex, "Silent Enforcer")

Cultist Magic User   CR 5
XP 1,600
hp 33 (Pathfinder Roleplaying Game GameMastery Guide, "Battle Mage")

Cultist Monk (20)CR 4
XP 1,200
hp 31 (Pathfinder Roleplaying Game NPC Codex, "Cruel Devotee")

If questioned, any captured cultists reveal that a handful of fellow cultists are in Mei Zhen. They were sent away from the great temple a few days ago and ordered not to return until summoned. Many among them believe they are being punished for failing their leader and goddess.

See the description of the cultists in Chapter Three for other information they may know.By the time the characters finish gathering the information, it is getting pretty late in the day. They may choose to accept Leigong's hospitality, in which case the night passes uneventfully. Or they may choose to get a head-start to their next destination.

Chapter Five:
The Fallen Temple

Long ago, *Nu3Wa1*, (Nuwa, mother goddess and creator of mankind), lived in a majestic palace built into the highest peaks of Heaven with her brother-husband *Fu2Xi1* (Fuxi, the emperor god).

An ancient tale tells of a great war between two great powers of Heaven. The losing side was cast into the underworld and banned from Heaven. The fallout from this war and exile caused the Four Pillars of Heaven to crumble.

Nuwa combined her magic with the color-stones and raised Heaven back into the skies. But this selfless act came at the cost of being unable to save her own place of power. Nuwa's palace fell deep into the underworld, and with it, the remaining cache of color-stones she had painstakingly sought. The cataclysmic clash of powers placed everything in the palace and around it in temporal stasis.

Crystal Legends

According to legend and myth, Nuwa quested across the known worlds and gathered a cache of magical color-stones. These are believed to be akin to magical versions of crystals amethysts, azurites, quartz, jasper, obsidian, turquoise, etc. She smelted five of these magical crystals together to fix the Four Pillars of Heaven when they crumbled.

Mei Lan found a part of Nuwa's fallen palace by sheer luck and saw her opportunity to use its power. Wanting to keep a close eye on Fei Du and the disciples, she convinced the cult to upgrade from their abandoned farmhouses into the fallen palace.

When the cultists returned without Niu Tian Shen, Mei Lan took his blood from their weapons and sent the cultists away. She's harnessing the power of Nuwa's remaining cache of colored-stones to siphon her husband's lifeforce for her own ends. To ensure she wouldn't be disturbed, Mei Lan used her magic to awaken underworld energies and beings best left alone.

Fei Du didn't leave with the other cultists; instead, she locked herself in her room.

Only a small wing of Nuwa's fallen palace is accessible during this adventure. The remainder is buried or destroyed.

There are two entrances to the fallen palace, one through a coal pit and the other a magic doorway used by the cultists. The characters can learn about either of these entrances from miners in Mei Zhen, and interrogating the cultists might lead directly to the cultists' entrance.

The Coal Pit

If the characters investigate the coal pit mentioned by the Elderly Miner in Mei Zhen, they find signs hammered into the ground starting at about a quarter mile out. Most of the signs have no writing but are configured to warn of danger or cursed lands ahead. Unlit red lanterns hang off poles erected near the path to scare away evil. There's even a shrine to the ancestors and the dead on the town's side of the red lantern perimeter.

> You find the abandoned mining pit surprisingly intact. The 15-foot-diameter pit's pulley system and rope are still attached at the top. With a quick glance down the hole, you see a small wooden landing wedged into the wall of the pit about 30 feet down. The remainder of the pit goes too deep for your eyes to see.

The characters must lower themselves a total of 300 feet before they hit bottom. They find a new wooden landing every 30 feet but each one is big enough only for one person to stand on at a time. The platforms have a 20% chance of breaking under characters whose total weight exceeds 250 lbs.

Occasionally, the characters discover small alcoves and other irregularities in the shaft, but none of these are full side passages or tunnels. Some are big enough for a character to stand or even sit inside if needed.

Once characters descend past 200 feet, 4 **coal demons** pull themselves from the walls and attack.

Coal Demon (4)   CR 3
XP 800
hp 16 (Tome of Horrors Complete, "Mephit, Smoke")

Remove Speed Fly (50 ft.); **Add Speed** Burrow (50 ft.)

If any of the characters is holding onto the walls, the coal demons burrow into the earth and push upward under their grip, burning their hands and possibly causing them to release their hold.

If characters are flying, the coal demons simply jump across the pit to grab them. These creatures are not afraid of falling because they simply catch the walls as they fall and burrow inward, emerging where they choose.

Read the following once characters reach the bottom of the pit:

> The warm, muggy air down here smells mildly of mildew, dirt, and dust. A tunnel opens to the east. Following it for a short distance, you see bits of roof shale and painted stone embedded in the walls, ceiling, and floor of the otherwise natural stone and dirt tunnel.

The roof shale and painted stone are very unusual to find in mines or caverns. These pieces come from Nuwa's palace and the other Heavenly buildings that fell during the collapse of the four pillars. Dwarves notice that the characters are definitely descending into the earth.

> A foul stench of rot and feces wafts to your nostrils.

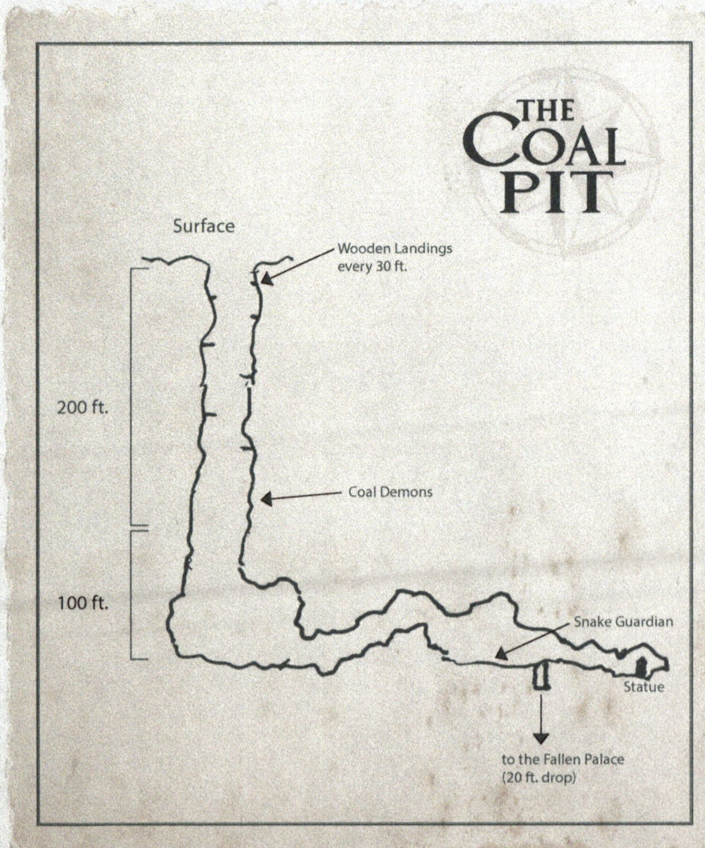

Give the characters some time to react, prepare, and maybe even get the jump on the snake ahead.

Once a guardian of Nuwa's palace, this **fiendish seven-headed divine guardian hydra** fell into the depths of the underworld with the palace and was corrupted. The snake doesn't have any treasure.

Fiendish Divine Guardian Hydra, Seven-headed   **CR 6**
XP 2,400
hp 67 (Appendix C: New Monsters, "Fiendish Divine Guardian Hydra, Seven-headed")

If the fallen guardian is defeated, the characters can discover a 20-foot-deep hole in the tunnel floor. The hole is more than five feet in diameter and worn smooth from the snake traveling in and out. If the characters continue exploring the tunnel before they drop down, they quickly find that it dead-ends at a crumpled wall near the remains of a statue.

The statue was once two snake tails intertwined with the upper bodies of a man and a woman facing each other. Now, it is split down the middle with the man and woman falling to opposite sides. The arms and parts of their heads are shattered, and large portions of the tail disappear into the cavern and crumpled wall.

Characters who drop down the hole land on the rooftop of the worship hall (Area **10**). A nest with five four-foot-tall eggs is on this rooftop. Three are intact but two are only broken shells. These eggs were laid hundreds of years ago.

Cultist Entrance

Searching the surface of the rock wall reveals a small, one-inch-diameter indentation where a chop could fit. Mei Lan installed this magical doorway for the cultists to travel to and from Nuwa's fallen palace. Every supplicant must wear his or her chop in order to pass through the doorway.

This portal radiates conjuration magic. Characters cannot see what is on the other side. Characters who step through find themselves outside the wing entrance (Area **B-1**) of Nuwa's Fallen Palace.

Area B: Nuwa's Fallen Palace

B-1. Wing Entrance

If the characters use the cultists' keys to enter, they are dimensionally teleported here.

B2. through B6. Servants' Quarters

These five rooms share the same general description with only a few minor changes.

The bundles at the foot of each bed include a change of clothes, an empty rice bowl, chopsticks, and a concealed weapon harness. The clothes belong to the cultists. Characters may use them as disguises if they desire. Characters also find six whetstones in the room.

A sketchbook someone has secretly been keeping is hidden under a floorboard beneath a cot in one of the rooms. All the art is drawn with coal dust, and most depict the same three people. The two men and one woman all appear to be in their late 20s to early 30s. Most of the pieces depict them fishing or down by the river. One stands out from the rest and shows the three sitting down for a tea ceremony.

Stuffed into one of the straw cots is a handful of miscellaneous jade jewelry.

Nuwa's Fallen Palace
B-14
B-12
B-13
B-9
B-10
B-11
B-8
B-7
B-6
B-5
B-4
B-3
B-2
B-1
N
E
S
W
1 Square - 5 Feet

Read the following when characters leave the second room:

Each character can react but unless they have powerful destructive magic such as *fireball*, they are unable to destroy the enchanted linens whirling around in the air about them. If they do have such magic, the encounter ends when the floating sheets are destroyed.

After each character reacts, the fabric ceases dancing and falls to the ground, forming into fashionable robes draped over a dozen beautiful men and women.

These **underworld phantasms** start by casting *charm person* on a couple of the characters they feel most receptive. They ply the characters with kindness, food, drink, and promise their heart's desires. The food and drink leave the characters in an altered state of mind and oblivious to anything but the party.

Characters who maintain their wits are attacked. The scene around these characters darkens, and the majority of the people in the room simply fade away.

Underworld Phantasm (12)   **CR 9**
XP 6,400
hp 90 (Appendix C: New Monsters, "Underworld Phantasm")

B-7. INNER DOOR

This is the inner door of the palace wing and separates the servants' quarters from Nuwa's inner sanctum. The walls on either side of this door are painted with murals of a snake-bodied creature with a human torso and head. The being is defeating a variety of monsters. The snake's body moves across several scenes, weaving between the monsters. The mural is in disrepair from age and the fall from Heaven.

B-8. OUTER COURTYARD

Some of the black metal cages (equivalent to cold iron) hanging over the courtyard detect of magic. A large pile of ash is off to one corner of the courtyard. Investigating it reveals small remnants of furniture. The cultists piled rotting and broken furniture from various rooms here and burned the heap.

Characters searching for the whimpering soul find a white fox named *Bi4Shou3* (Bishou, "Monarch's Hand") in one of the square cages. The fox is wounded and weak. A strange crank is on the outside of the magical cage, but nothing is visible that should stop the fox from squeezing between the bars.

This crank was used to shrink the cage, which forced Bishou to shift from his human form to that of the fox. The handle can be cranked in the opposite direction to make the cage up to three times bigger, which is enough space for a human.

Bishou can speak while in animal form, but he currently has large blanks in his memory. He feels as if his memory is actively slipping away while he talks with the characters. He's been focusing on remembering his mission to retrieve something belonging to his lord. Yet he cannot remember his lord's name or the item.

He knows that the mission is very important, and that the fate of many souls is on the line. He knows that many humans have come and gone while he has been in the cage. Recently, all but one of them left.

The cage leeches Bishou's magical powers and creates a feedback field that prevents him from teleporting out or squeezing between the bars. Bishou's Heavenly soldier nature is directly oppositional to the place in which he's being kept, so it is slowly draining away his self-identity and his memories.

Characters can pick the lock of the cage to release Bishou with a successful DC 20 Disable Device check. The magic doesn't prevent tampering from the outside of the cage.

Bishou has a sandy-colored birthmark shaped like a gourd just below his neck on the front of his chest. The blood of mortals, including the blood in this courtyard, burns the white fox on contact and lights his fur on fire. He takes 1d6 damage every round until the blood is washed off and the fire is put out.

Bishou   CR 6
XP 2,400
hp 59 (Pathfinder Roleplaying Game Bestiary 2, "Vulpinal")

Two of the cages house miners from the search party that was sent after the first group of miners who went missing. They are dehydrated and starving but can be healed and questioned. Their cages have inward-facing spikes along the walls and roofs. Their names are *Tu3An1* (Tuan, "Peaceful Earth") and *Gu3Dong4* (Gudong, "Drum in Motion"). Both miners beg the characters to release them from the cages and take them back to Mei Zhen.

Tuan saw other prisoners taken away, never to return. But the cultists stopped taking people days, maybe weeks, ago. He doesn't have an exact count of days because there's no real sense of time down here. He doesn't know why they stopped, but he's certain the reprieve won't last forever.

They've seen the cultists come and go and believe their leader is someone named Fei Du. They've only seen her once or twice, but she mentioned that her patron ordered the feedings be put on hold. They don't know what that means.

Gudong recalls that a group of cultists came through recently. They carried bloody weapons and took a girl into the big two-story building. They exited without their weapons and the girl. He thinks he passed out for a while but remembers waking up later when all the cultists were leaving.

Gudong hasn't seen Fei Du since that day, so he guesses she left with the cultists.

Another cage has earth and fire sprites packed tightly together. They're weak but when the characters approach, they stomp and buzz about trying to communicate. The cage radiates magic, and the sprites bounce against some sort of forcefield between the bars. Characters cannot communicate with them unless they share an elemental language or have some magical means to do so. The cultists captured the sprites, and the cult leader was "eating" them by sucking their souls into a magical gourd and then drinking the soul from the gourd. She recently stopped, but they don't know why.

At some point while the characters are investigating the cages, the fresh blood pools rise up as 2 **blood golems** and attack. These creatures are formed from the corruption in the area combined with Mei Lan's powers.

Hua Yue is not in any of the cages.

Blood Golem (2) CR 6
XP 2,400
hp 64 (Pathfinder Roleplaying Game Bestiary 4, "Golem, Blood")

B-9. Fei Du's Sanctum

> Whatever this room once was, it has been transformed into a luxurious bedroom. White lanterns and a handful of candles provide light but also fill areas of the room with dancing shadows.
>
> A sickly-sweet perfume hangs oppressively in the air, mixed with the spicy scent of cinnamon and lightly musty machilus wood. There are polished redwood tables, stools, a bed, and a vanity, all engraved and carved with intricate designs of various winged creatures. Red, silk-covered pillows and sheets are embroidered with similar winged creatures in gold, white, and blue thread.
>
> A woman sits cross legged on the floor in front of a scholar's desk. She has pale skin marred by black veins that pulse up her neck and face. Her eyes are flooded with blood. She's gracefully holding one sleeve back and writing in an open scroll. She slides a well-manicured index finger up her brush and gestures for you to wait. She writes one more word and leans down to blow a greenish-gray breath across the paper before rolling the scroll closed.

Fei Du is in the process of losing her soul and transforming into a monster. She is currently penning the saga of her rise to immortality and godhood. She is egotistical and delusional. She believes she's ascending, when in reality all her experiments and practices caused her to twist and mutate into a poisonous mogui.

If the characters play to her ego, she offers them tea and tells them her story, expecting to gain more worshippers. Unbeknownst to Fei Du, her fingernails are envenomed. Measuring the tea leaves infuses them with poison. Characters who drink the tea must make a DC 14 Fortitude save versus poison. If they fail, black veins spread across their skin and start choking them to death.

Fei Du's Poison
Type poison, ingested; **Save** Fortitude DC 14; **Onset** 1 round;
    Frequency 1/round for 6 rounds; **Cure** 2 consecutive saves
Effect 1d4 Strength damage. A creature reduced to 0 Strength by the
    poison asphyxiates and immediately begins suffocating. Creatures
    that do not breathe are immune to this suffocation, but not the
    Strength damage.

See the adventure background for details about her history.

Fei Du will answer a few questions:

* Hua Yue is still alive. "That little thief stole a heart that doesn't belong to her. Now she's going to give back his gift if it's the last thing she does. My goddess will see to that and reward me for my service while punishing his betrayal."

* She believes she will ascend to take over for Niu Tian Shen once he's removed from the picture. Niu Tian Shen didn't understand his place, so he doesn't deserve to keep it.

Characters may circumvent this fight by turning Fei Du against her patron goddess. If she can be convinced that Mei Lan is not going to hold up her end of the deal, she joins the characters in confronting the goddess.

Fei Du wears expensive green robes embroidered all over with winged creatures. Half her hair is pinned up with several jade, gold, and pearl accessories. The black veins spreading across her skin and her long green fingernails contrast sharply with her pale features.
During a fight, she flings out her robes and casts a *stinking cloud* centered on her (to which she is immune).

She fights and parries with two poisoned cultist daggers. Her fighting style uses her robes, specifically her sleeves, to hide where her attacks are coming from. This allows her to feint with a +2 circumstance bonus.

Fei Du   CR 8
XP 4,800
hp 58 (Appendix C: New Monsters, "Fei Du")

Once characters deal with Fei Du, they have free rein to search her room. A redwood altar box with orchids carved into its ivory door panels is in a dark corner on the opposite side of the room from the bed. Wisps of incense float from the negative spaces between the carvings. (Ivory is extremely rare because of the region's Taoist and Buddhist culture. Sourcing ivory would normally be from an animal that died of natural causes.)

Characters who open the box find:

- Several wooden panels painted with various colors of orchid flowers.
- A gold statue of a beautiful woman dressed in long flowing robes standing on an open orchid flower. Her robes are engraved with orchids that are filled in with colored dyes.
- An offering of peaches and oranges in a jade bowl with two dragons carved on opposite sides. The lip of the bowl is so thin that light passes through it. Characters who eat the offerings bring bad luck on themselves. They are forced to reroll their first successful die roll against Mei Lan and keep the new result.

A gold incense bowl in the room is filled with sand and holds three sticks of still-burning incense. It's clear that this is where the strong smell of cinnamon and machilus wood is coming from.

A secret compartment in the bed that contains the soul gourd the white fox Bishou was sent to retrieve can be found with a successful DC 20 Perception check. The soul gourd detects of powerful magic.

The mirror on the vanity shows each character not as they look but as they wish to see themselves. It was a gift to Fei Du from Mei Lan so she wouldn't see what she was actually becoming.

Inside the drawers of the vanity, characters find jewelry and some makeup. Included in the jewelry is a complicated decorative knot linked with three coins. It radiates magic and functions as a *brooch of shielding* with 3d4 x 10 points of protection (max 101) on it before unraveling itself.

A sharpened hairpin functions as a *+1 frost returning dart*.

B-10. Worship Hall

This room is two stories tall with the second story being an internal balcony with staircases leading up from two sides. An eight-foot-tall wooden statue in the center of the far wall is of the same beautiful woman as found in the altar box in Fei Du's sanctum (Area **B-9**), complete with her standing on an orchid. The flooring appears to be made of some sort of packed clay. Otherwise, the room is empty.

Characters who go upstairs find that the stairs are rickety and not maintained, requiring a DC 15 Acrobatics or Climb check to avoid falling through. Boards may break off. Characters who successfully make it to the top find themselves breaking through brittle and weak flooring. The wood is infested with the same blight as the furniture that the cultists piled up and burned.

B-11. Mess Hall

This room is mostly empty, with only some straw mats covered in linen left for seating around the room. Characters can find a large bucket containing empty bowls, several jars of fermented food items, and a bamboo box filled with cold, cooked rice.

B-12. and B-13. Collapsed Buildings and Inner Courtyard

This area is pitch black. Characters must provide their own light sources or have darkvision to compensate.

These aren't statues. They are actually underworld creatures in stasis caused by the magical fallout when the palace fell from Heaven. Mei Lan's ritual is waking them.

When the characters reach the middle of the inner courtyard, they start to hear the rumbling of earth and feel minor tremors in the ground beneath their feet. The creatures are pulling themselves free.

The 2 **blue-skinned devils** come to life and attack.

Blue-skinned Devil (2)   CR 8
XP 4,800
hp 92 (Pathfinder Roleplaying Game Bestiary, "Oni, Ogre Mage")

Remove Gear All; **Add Attack 4** Claws +15 (1d6 + 7)

B-14. Nuwa's Fallen Sanctum

This is where Nuwa stored her cache of color-stones.

The woman on the throne is Mei Lan, while Hua Yue sits on the floor. If the characters attack Mei Lan, Hua Yue throws herself in the way and calls out to the group. She claims that Mei Lan is just trying to save her husband.

Hua Yue is under the effects of a *charm person* spell cast by Mei Lan. This causes Hua Yue to believe Mei Lan is her trusted best friend and will behave accordingly. It is important to understand that Hua Yue's nature and motivations are still accessible to the characters.

Mei Lan is not completely evil, yet. She is lovesick and her perspective on the world has been warped with time and her powers. If she isn't set on a different course soon, Leigong or another Heavenly soldier is likely to be sent to remove her from existence.

She has no interest in fighting the characters. She has convinced Hua Yue that she must return the *xiao* to Niu Tian Shen so that he can be healed and made whole.

If Fei Du is with the characters, she accuses Mei Lan of tricking and using her. She is quite open about her version of what happened. She has done everything Mei Lan asked of her, including pausing her experiments on the prisoners.

In the hands of the rightful owner, the xiao can summon Niu Tian Shen. If this happens, Mei Lan has medicine prepared to heal him once he's made whole. Secretly, Mei Lan also intends to dose her husband with a cup of Meng Po's five-flavored tea of forgetfulness for a fresh start to their relationship.

> *Meng Po is the goddess of the afterlife. She serves a special soup on the Bridge of Forgetfulness to wipe a person's memory before they step into the afterlife or are reincarnated. She waits for dead souls at the entrance to the ninth realm of the dead.*
>
> *Alternatively, she is known for collecting various herbs from earthly ponds and streams to make her five-flavored tea of forgetfulness. This tea is given to each soul to drink before they leave the underworld. The tea causes immediate and permanent amnesia as it wipes away all memories of their past lives.*

Mei Lan and Niu Tian Shen were married through an arranged marriage. She fell madly in love with Niu Tian Shen, while he eventually grew to love her. Still, they struggled to get along; it was a volatile relationship with poor communication. Eventually, the two agreed to live separate lives. Since then, Niu Tian Shen has avoided the mountains where his wife resides.

If asked about her association with the cultists, she expresses embarrassment. "I let jealousy get the best of me, I'll admit."

Mei Lan claims that the cultists were doing some very evil things before she came around. She put a stop to it and was helping them seek redemption. She actually did stop the cultists from continuing their murder spree, which is something hinted at by prisoners in the outer courtyard (area **B-8**). Mei Lan figured that if she couldn't redeem Fei Du and the cultists, she would turn them over for judgement.

Characters can point out that she used her knowledge and powers to cause harm to humans and spirits. She initially denies this, but can be persuaded to see the truth.

Characters may notice during the conversation that the crystals seem to be activated for some sort of siphoning ritual with a successful DC 20 Knowledge (arcana) check. If confronted about this, Mei Lan explains she was trying to save her husband's essence because she didn't know how else to retrieve his horn or summon him.

If any characters knowledgeable in poison took the remnants of zhenniao feathers from the provincial roadhouse and concocted their own poison dose, it can be used against Mei Lan. If Mei Lan fails a DC 20 Fortitude saving throw, she suffers a 20% failure rate on her spellcasting due to confusion caused by the toxin.

Mei Lan CR 9
XP 6,400
hp 82 (Appendix C: New Monsters, "Mei Lan")

If her hit points drops below 20%, she teleports away with a parting curse under her breath (if reduced to 0 hit points, her contingent teleport lets her escape). Characters earn her ire. She ends up somewhere gravely wounded and very peeved

CONCLUDING THE ADVENTURE

After characters talk sense into Mei Lan or defeat her in combat, they can find a bloodstained knife that is being used to siphon Niu Tian Shen's lifeforce. The blade is embedded in a color-stone. Pulling the knife from the color-stone disrupts the ritual and returns Niu Tian Shen to normal (see below).

Hua Yue can summon Niu Tian Shen by playing the xiao. She's then able to return his horn, which fuses back into place.

Several options for concluding the adventure include but are not limited to:

MEI LAN AND NIU TIAN SHEN ARE REUNITED

Niu Tian Shen is healed, but his memory has also been erased. Mei Lan uses this opportunity to build a new reality and a new beginning for them. Niu Tian Shen and Mei Lan renew their marital vows, and he moves into the mountains with her.

Unfortunately, this leaves Niu Tian Shen only tenuously tied to his domain. Agriculture in the region suffer for years, and the land won't be able to support the current population. A significant recession occurs.

If characters don't rescue Hua Yue, she disappears, never to be heard from again.

NIU TIAN SHEN IS REUNITED WITH HIS TRUE LOVE, HUA YUE

Once Niu Tian Shen is made whole, characters can heal him with their magic. The lands are revitalized and heal before the night of Qixi.

FEI DU IS SET ON A PATH OF REDEMPTION

Fei Du is open to suggestions on how to redeem herself. If the characters don't direct her path, she seeks out Lord Wu and begs him to allow her to serve him in penance.

THE CHARACTERS WALKED AWAY FROM THE ADVENTURE OR DIDN'T FINISH BEFORE THE NIGHT OF QIXI

The lands continue to die. On the night of Qixi, Mei Lan's siphoning ritual consumes Niu Tian Shen's soul, which severs his connection with the land. She feeds him Meng Po's five-flavored tea of forgetfulness and takes him away to her home in the skies.

Within days, the lands start wasting away to desert. Fei Du rises as a dark lord of the land.

Appendix A: Names and Phrases

Names and phrases in Chinese often have multiple meanings because the spoken word can have multiple ways to write it; the different written characters have different meanings. This wordplay is used in this module with characters such as Fei Du, which means Flight and Read/Study, but written differently can mean Fragrant Poison. The following tables contains some common words and phrases you can use in the adventure, as well as the names and meanings of various NPCs.

Names

Name	Phonetic Writing	English
牛天神	Niu Tian Shen	Ox Lord of New Day's Toil
美蘭	Mei Lan	Beautiful Orchard
飛讀/緋毒	Fei Du	Flight & Study/Fragrant Poison
嫿月	Hua Yue	Tranquil Moon
毋	Wu	"Nobody" (Surname Form)
辟手/庇手	Bishou	Monarch's Hand/Sheltering Hand (Protector)
土安	Tuan	Peaceful Earth
鼓動	Gudong	Drum in Motion
煤鎮/梅鎮	Mei Zhen	Coal Town/Plum Flower Town
謂風	Weifeng	Reason's Wind
雷公	Leigong	God of Thunder
洋	Yang	Ocean, Vast, Silver Coin, Foreign

Phrases

Chinese	Phonetic Writing	English
你好	Ni³ Hao³	Hello (informal)
您好	Nin² Hao³	Hello (formal)
再見	Zai⁴jian⁴	Goodbye
謝謝	Xie⁴xie	Thank you
不客氣	Bu⁴ke⁴qi	You're welcome
歡迎光臨	Huan¹ying²guang¹lin²	Welcome (in the context of hospitality)
走了	Zou³ Le	Gone away (through movement)
多少錢	Duo¹ Shao³ Qian²	How much money?
來了	Lai²le	Arriving/Coming!

Appendix B: New Items

Day of the Seven Cranes

Aura strong abjuration; **CL** 17th; **Slot** —; **Price** 5,000 gp; **Weight** 5 lbs.

Characters who flip through the book see diagrams of motion and notes about focusing and channeling one's lifeforce to direct certain outcomes. Many of the poses and motions reflect the movements of a crane in flight and on land.

A character may study the martial practices within this manual for one week, excluding all activity other than eating, sleeping, and training. At the end of a week, they gain a +1 inherent bonus to their AC due to the defensive maneuvers they learn. This bonus to AC fades if they do not practice their training each day for at least one uninterrupted hour while using the manual as a reference. The manual can provide this bonus only to one creature at a time. If training is not performed for more than a week, a character must restart their one-week training with the book, or another character can begin their own study.

Feats Craft Wondrous Item, *miracle* or *wish*; **Cost** 2,500 gp

Hua Yue's Xiao (Minor Artifact)

This is a vertical end-blown flute bearing a scene of a woman dancing her way to the mountains skillfully carved into the material. It is made from the horn of Niu Tian Shen.

Successfully playing the instrument does two things:

* Calms the maddened Niu Tian Shen. (This is important if characters track him down later in the adventure.)

* Manifests a vision based on the song played. If the characters play a sad ballad, they call forth a vision of the attack at the provincial roadhouse. Characters can manifest other visions when playing music, depending on the song. With time, the characters may even learn to control how the visions manifest.

Soul Gourd (Minor Artifact)

Bottle gourds have many magical and symbolic references. From being Taoist Fulu charms to bottle gourds being holding magical elixirs, and even myths of Bottle Gourds being portals to another world.

In the case of the Soul Gourd, it is a magical artifact that is able to trap souls and allow them to be drunk as elixirs.

Spirit Money

Spirit money is not technically a magic item, but it is a means of connecting with the spirit world.

Spirit money (also known as Hell money, incense paper, or joss paper) is burned for the dead or for mystical beings to ensure that they are well taken care of in the spirit world. Sometimes, objects fashioned out of this special paper — such as paper jewelry, clothes, or furniture — are burned as offerings.

Zhenniao Poison

Zhenniao are daemon birds with varied reports on their appearance. The most common stories describe them as a cross between a peacock and a crane. They are extremely poisonous, from beak to feather. Lore speaks of their venom coming from the poisonous vipers that make up the bulk of these unique birds' diets. The poison's interaction with the birds' chemistry concentrates and mutates the viper poison, infusing the birds from beak to tail feathers. One bite of their meat is said to cause instant death in a human.

While no known antidote or cure exists in the mortal world, lore speaks of neutralizing the toxin using a great rhino horn but only if the poison isn't yet in the bloodstream.

Appendix C: New Monsters

Canker Vines

These vines grow around themselves and resemble woven rope. Canker vines feed on life and can sense living Chi. They attack only living creatures, never undead or objects. These vines tend to grow around 30 to 60 feet long when bundled together.

When attacking, the vines open and extend outward like many tendrils to completely engulf the target. Boils of black ichor surface along the lengths of each individual vine and burst against the skin of the living, acting as a sedative and corrosive acid. The vines strangle and suffocate incapacitated victims.

Canker Vine   CR 8

XP 4,800
Unique canopy creeper
NE Huge plant
Init +7; **Senses** lifesense, low-light vision; Perception +13
AC 23, touch 11, flat-footed 20 (+3 Dex, +12 natural, -2 size)
hp 150 (12d8+96); fast healing 2
Fort +16, **Ref** +9, **Will** +4
Immune electricity, mind-affecting effects, paralysis, poison, polymorph, sleep, stunning; **Resist** fire 10
Weaknesses vulnerability to cold
Speed 10 ft., climb 20 ft.
Melee bite +15 (2d6 + 12)
Ranged 4 vine tendrils +10 (grab plus feed plus pull)
Space 15 ft.; **Reach** 10 ft.
Special Attacks aquatic attack, feed, pull (30 ft.)
Str 26, **Dex** 16, **Con** 26, **Int** 2, **Wis** 10, **Cha** 10
Base Atk +9; **CMB** +19 (+23 grapple); **CMD** 32 (can't be tripped)
Feats Blind-fight, Combat Reflexes, Improved Initiative, Lightning Reflexes, Multiattack, Skill Focus (Climb)
Skills Acrobatics +3 (-5 to jump), Climb +19, Perception +13, Stealth +4 (+20 in water); **Racial Modifiers** Perception +4, Stealth +16 in water
SQ camouflage, vine tendrils
Special Abilities
Aquatic Attack (Ex) +2 bonus on attack rolls when battling a creature that is in water.
Camouflage (Ex) Because a canker vine blends in with the foliage that is its natural habitat, a DC 20 Perception check (modified for distance) is required to notice it before it attacks for the first time. Any creature with ranks in Survival or Knowledge (nature) can use either of those skills (also modified for distance) instead of Perception to notice the plant.
Feed (Ex) Grappled creature take 1d8 + 1 Strength damage.
Vine Tendrils (Ex) A canker vine can take control of any network of vines it has attached itself to and use up to four of those vines as weapons to strike out at targets up to 100 feet away. The vine tendrils have 10 hit points, DR 5 / slashing, and a Break DC of 21. If one of these vines is destroyed, the canopy creeper can assume control of another vine as a move action to bring it to bear in combat.

Fiendish Divine Guardian Hydra, Seven-Headed

This seven-headed snake was a guardian of humanity but the fall of Nuwa's palace into the underworld allowed darkness and corruption to seep into its very essence. While the snake's various bites hurt its foes, the injected venom is a bigger danger. The snake likes to "ferment" its meals by letting its victims die slowly due to injury and paralysis; it swallows them whole at a later date.

Fiendish Divine Guardian Hydra, Seven-Headed   CR 6

XP 2,400
NE Huge magical beast (evil)
Init +5; **Senses** darkvision 60 ft., low-light vision, scent; Perception +19
AC 17, touch 9, flat-footed 16 (+1 Dex, +8 natural, -2 size)
hp 67 (7d10+28); fast healing 7
Fort +9, **Ref** +8, **Will** +6
Defensive Abilities ability healing; **DR** 5/good; **Immune** disease, mind-affecting effects, poison; **Resist** cold 10, fire 10; **SR** 11
Speed 40 ft., swim 20 ft.
Melee 7 bites +8 (1d8 + 3 plus poison)
Space 15 ft.; **Reach** 10 ft.
Special Attacks poison, pounce, smite good
Spell-Like Abilities (CL 7th; concentration +9)
  At will—*dimension door* (within sacred site only)
  3/day—*alarm, knock*
  1/day—*arcane lock, augury, clairaudience / clairvoyance, dismissal* (DC 17), *hold portal*
Str 17, **Dex** 12, **Con** 18, **Int** 6, **Wis** 15, **Cha** 14
Base Atk +7; **CMB** +12; **CMD** 23 (can't be tripped)
Feats Combat Reflexes, Iron Will, Lightning Reflexes, Power Attack
Skills Acrobatics +1 (+5 to jump), Perception +19, Sense Motive +7, Swim +11; **Racial Modifiers** +7 Perception, +5 Sense Motive
SQ blessed life, divine swiftness, hydra traits, regenerate head, sacred site
Special Abilities
Ability Healing (Ex) A divine guardian heals 1 point of ability damage per round in each damaged ability score.
Blessed Life (Ex) A divine guardian does not age or breathe. It does not require food, drink, or sleep.
Divine Swiftness (Ex) A divine guardian is gifted with incredible speed, granting it a +4 bonus on initiative rolls. In addition, each of the base creature's speeds are doubled. If the base creature has a fly speed, the divine guardian's maneuverability becomes perfect if it was not already. If the divine guardian acquires the air, earth, or water subtype, it gains a fly, burrow, or swim speed equal to its highest speed.
Hydra Traits (Ex) A hydra can be killed by severing all of its heads or slaying its body. Any attack that is not an attempt to sever a head affects the body, including area attacks or attacks that cause piercing or bludgeoning damage. To sever a head, an opponent must make a sunder attempt with a slashing weapon targeting a head. A head is considered a separate weapon with hardness 0 and hit points equal to the hydra's HD. To sever a head, an opponent must inflict enough damage to reduce the head's hit points to 0 or less. Severing a head deals damage to the hydra's body equal to the hydra's current HD. A hydra can't attack with a severed head, but takes no other penalties.
Poison: - Injury (DC 17) (Ex) Poison—Injury; save Fort DC 17; frequency 1 / round 4 rounds; effect paralysis for 1d4 rounds; cure 1 save.
Regenerate Head (Ex) When a hydra's head is destroyed, two heads regrow in 1d4 rounds. A hydra cannot have more than twice its original number of heads at any one time. To prevent new heads from growing, at least 5 points of acid or fire damage must be dealt to the stump (a touch attack to hit) before they appear. Acid or fire damage from area attacks can affect stumps and the body simultaneously. A hydra doesn't die from losing its heads until all are cut off and the stumps seared by acid or fire.

Sacred Site (Ex) Each divine guardian is assigned to guard a specific site sacred to the deity that invested it with power. This area may be a structure, a series of structures, or a natural site with clearly defined borders. It can be as large as a city, but in most cases it's a single temple or a sacred grove. Gods don't waste their powers on places that their worshipers can protect, so most divine guardians keep watch over abandoned burial grounds or lost temples. The divine guardian of such a site is charged with protecting it from harm and preventing incursions by those not of the faith. It must keep its vigil until the god deems the guardian's task done.

If the divine guardian ever moves out of the area defined as the sacred site, it immediately loses the divine guardian template and any spellcasting ability the deity might have granted from class levels. It cannot regain the template unless it atones for its failure (usually by completing some quest or via an *atonement* spell) and reenters the site within 1 week. Otherwise, it loses the template permanently, taking 6d6 points of Constitution drain as the years of lost food, drink, and sleep return to it tenfold. A creature that lacks a Constitution score takes 2d6 points of damage per Hit Die from this process. Even if it survives the Constitution drain, the creature can never regain the template.

Smite Good (1/day) (Su) +2 to hit, +7 to damage when used.

FETID HANDS

Formed of rotting tree bark and insects, these hands are in constant "search" of something but cursed to never find what they seek or at least not to realize it when they find it.

FETID HANDS SWARM   CR 1

XP 400
NE Fine undead (swarm)
Init +1; **Senses** blindsense 30 ft., darkvision 60 ft.; Perception +4
AC 19, touch 19, flat-footed 18 (+1 Dex, +8 size)
hp 9 (1d8+5)
Fort +2, **Ref** +1, **Will** +2
Defensive Abilities swarm traits; **Immune** undead traits
Speed 40 ft., climb 40 ft.
Melee swarm (1d6 plus grab)
Space 10 ft.; **Reach** 0 ft.
Special Attacks distraction (DC 12), mark quarry, strangle
Str 13, **Dex** 13, **Con** —, **Int** 2, **Wis** 11, **Cha** 14
Base Atk +0; **CMB** —; **CMD** —
Feats Toughness
Skills Acrobatics +1 (+5 to jump), Climb +9, Perception +4, Survival +4; **Racial Modifiers** +4 Survival
Languages Common (can't speak)
Special Abilities
Distraction (DC 12) (Ex) Nauseate foes for 1 round on failed save. (Fort neg.)
Mark Quarry (designated quarry) (Su) A fetid hand swarm is assigned a quarry by anointing the hands with a drop of the intended quarry's blood. If the hands have no current quarry, they automatically gain the next creature they damage as their quarry. Once attuned to a target, they become aware of the target's location as if under the effect of a continuous *locate creature* spell. The hands gain a +1 bonus on all attack rolls, damage rolls, and skill checks made to seek out and destroy the marked quarry. The mark quarry ability lasts until the quarry or the hands are slain.
Strangle (Ex) Grappled foes cannot speak or cast spells with verbal components.

MEI LAN

Mei Lan starts by casting *dominate person* on the character with the biggest weapon or the one that is most heavily armored. She then commands that character to kill the rest of the group. She's an enchantment specialist but casts some volatile spells by flinging fulu scripts at her targets.

MEI LAN   CR 9

XP 6,400
CN Medium fey
Init +4; **Senses** low-light vision; Perception +19
AC 21, touch 15, flat-footed 16 (+4 Dex, +1 dodge, +6 natural)
hp 82 (15d6+30); regeneration 5 (fire or acid)
Fort +7, **Ref** +13, **Will** +10
DR 5/cold iron and magic
Speed 30 ft., fly 30 ft. (good)
Melee 2 claws +7 (1d4)
Spell-Like Abilities (CL 15th; concentration +20)
 At will—*charm person* (DC 16)
 3/day—*bestow curse* (DC 18), *deep slumber* (DC 18), *lightning bolt* (DC 18)
 1/day—*cone of cold* (DC 20), *dominate person* (DC 20), *teleport*
 1/week—*contingency*
Str 10, **Dex** 18, **Con** 15, **Int** 15, **Wis** 13, **Cha** 21
Base Atk +7; **CMB** +7; **CMD** 22
Feats Combat Expertise, Crane Style, Crane Wing, Deflect Arrows, Dodge, Improved Unarmed Strike, Redirect Attack, Snatch Arrows
Skills Bluff +23, Diplomacy +23, Fly +26, Knowledge (local) +20, Knowledge (nature) +20, Perception +19, Sense Motive +19, Use Magic Device +23
Languages Common, Sylvan

MOGWAI

FEI DU

Fei Du wears expensive green robes embroidered all over with winged creatures. Half her hair is pinned up with several jade, gold, and pearl accessories. The black veins spreading across her skin and her long green fingernails contrast sharply with her pale features.

FEI DU   CR 8

XP 4,800
NE Medium fey
Init +3; **Senses** low-light vision; Perception +16
AC 13, touch 13, flat-footed 10 (+3 Dex)
hp 58 (13d6+13)
Fort +5, **Ref** +11, **Will** +8
DR 5/magic and silver; **Immune** poison; **SR** 19
Speed 30 ft.
Melee *+1 injecting toxic virulent dagger* +5/+5/+0/+0 (1d4 + 1 plus poison [DC 20] /19-20) or
 +1 injecting toxic virulent dagger +7/+2 (1d4 + 1 plus poison [DC 20] /19-20)
Sorcerer Spells Known (CL 13th; concentration +16)
 6th (4/day)—*geas / quest, planar binding* (DC 19)
 5th (6/day)—*mass charm person* (DC 18), *dominate person* (DC 18), *teleport*
 4th (6/day)—*aggravate affliction, contingent venom* (DC 17), *miasmatic form, sword to snake* (DC 17)
 3rd (7/day)—*create soul gem* (DC 16), *ja noi aspect, nauseating trail* (DC 16), *stinking cloud* (DC 16)
 2nd (7/day)—*accelerate poison* (DC 15), *demand offering* (DC 15), *hidden blades, languid venom* (DC 15), *unnatural lust* (DC 15)
 1st (7/day)—*charm person* (DC 14), *mage armor, memory lapse* (DC 14), *obscure poison, poisoned egg*
 0 (at will)—*dancing lights, detect poison, ghost sound* (DC 13), *haunted fey aspect, mage hand, message, prestidigitation, read magic, touch of fatigue* (DC 13)
Str 11, **Dex** 17, **Con** 13, **Int** 14, **Wis** 10, **Cha** 17
Base Atk +6; **CMB** +6; **CMD** 19
Feats Combat Expertise, Greater Feint, Improved Feint, Improved

Two-weapon Fighting, Subtle Poisoner, Two-weapon Feint, Two-weapon Fighting

Skills Bluff +19, Diplomacy +19, Disguise +19, Perception +16, Sense Motive +16, Sleight of Hand +19, Stealth +19, Use Magic Device +19

Languages Aklo, Common, Sylvan

Combat Gear wyvern poison (10); **Other Gear** *+1 injecting toxic virulent dagger* (wyvern poison [3]), *+1 injecting toxic virulent dagger* (wyvern poison [3]), speed sheath (2)

Special Abilities

Greater Feint Feinted foe loses DEX until the beginning of your next turn, rather than on next attack.

Improved Feint You can make a Bluff check to feint in combat as a move action.

Subtle Poisoner You can apply poison as part of drawing a weapon.

Two-Weapon Feint Forgo first melee attack to feint

Wyvern Poison

Type poison (injury); **Save** Fortitude DC 17; **Frequency** 1/round for 6 rounds; **Cure** 2 consecutive saves

Effect 1d4 Con damage

Mogwai, Rot and Fecundity

Mei Gen

Mei Gen shoots green and black lightning bolts from his fingertips at a single target whenever there are 3 or more characters in a line. If the lightning strikes an area of the wall that doesn't already have fungus growing, fungus grows rapidly in the area. If he hits an area with existing fungus, spores release a cloud that obscures sight within a five-foot radius.

Between those rounds, he flies around the room clawing at the characters with his nasty, diseased nails. Each time his nails connect, the character must save against his Charisma draining poison.

Mogwai, Rot and Fecundity   CR 8

XP 4,800

NE Large outsider (giant, native, oni, shapechanger)

Init +7; **Senses** darkvision 60 ft., low-light vision; Perception +13

AC 17, touch 12, flat-footed 14 (+3 Dex, +5 natural, -1 size)

hp 92 (8d10+48); regeneration 5 (fire or acid)

Fort +12, **Ref** +5, **Will** +10

DR 5/magic and silver; **SR** 19

Speed 40 ft., fly 60 ft. (good)

Melee 2 claws +14 (1d6 + 7 plus poison)

Space 10 ft.; **Reach** 10 ft.

Special Attacks poison

Spell-Like Abilities (CL 8th; concentration +11)

Constant—*fly*

At will—*fungal blisters, grasping tentacles*

3/day—*lightning bolt* (DC 16)

1/day—*black tentacles*

Str 24, **Dex** 17, **Con** 23, **Int** 14, **Wis** 14, **Cha** 17

Base Atk +8; **CMB** +16; **CMD** 29

Feats Combat Expertise, Combat Reflexes, Improved Initiative, Iron Will

Skills Acrobatics +3 (+7 to jump), Bluff +14, Fly +16, Knowledge (nature) +13, Knowledge (planes) +13, Knowledge (religion) +13, Perception +13, Sense Motive +13, Spellcraft +13

Languages Aklo, Common, Giant, Sylvan

Special Abilities

Poison: - Injury (DC 20) (Ex) Poison—Injury; save Fort DC 20; frequency 1 / round 4 rounds; effect 1 Cha drain; cure 1 save.

Mogwai, Chi Thief

Qing Shan

Qing Shan is a rather common type of mogwai, a spirit returned to the land of the living that straddles life and death. When forced to confront their reality, they steal the chi of others in an attempt to return fully to the world of the living.

Chi thieves breathe in the chi of their targets. The range is often dependent on how powerful of a mogwai it is. In the case of Qing Shan, she grabs the head or neck of her target and breathes in.

Mogwai, Chi Thief   CR 4

XP 1,200

NE Medium undead (extraplanar, oni)

Init +1; **Senses** darkvision 60 ft.; Perception +9

AC 13, touch 11, flat-footed 12 (+1 Dex, +2 natural)

hp 37 (5d8+15)

Fort +4, **Ref** +2, **Will** +5

DR 5 / magic and silver; **Immune** undead traits

Speed 30 ft.

Melee slam +3 (1d4), touch +3 (1 plus energy drain)

Special Attacks energy drain (one level, DC 15)

Str 10, **Dex** 13, **Con** —, **Int** 13, **Wis** 12, **Cha** 17

Base Atk +3; **CMB** +3; **CMD** 14

Feats Combat Expertise, Combat Reflexes, Stand Still

Skills Disguise +11, Knowledge (arcana) +9, Knowledge (religion) +9, Perception +9, Sense Motive +9

Languages Common, Necronomus

SQ rejuvenation

Special Abilities

Rejuvenation (Su) A slain chi thief mogwai returns to unlife at full hit points at the next sundown. On the anniversary of its wrongful death, a chi thief mogwai reforms 1 hour after it is reduced to 0 hit points. The only way to destroy a chi thief mogwai is to bring to light the true offender or lay the spirit to rest with a ritual.

Mogwai, Chi Thief — Incorporeal Form

A chi thief possesses a suitable living host and waits for an opportune time to suck the chi out of unsuspecting people.

Mogwai, Chi Thief (incorporeal form)   CR 4

XP 1,200

NE Medium undead (extraplanar, incorporeal, oni)

Init +1; **Senses** darkvision 60 ft.; Perception +9

AC 14, touch 14, flat-footed 13 (+3 deflection, +1 Dex)

hp 37 (5d8+15)

Fort +4, **Ref** +2, **Will** +5

Defensive Abilities incorporeal; **DR** 5/magic and silver; **Immune** undead traits

Speed 30 ft.

Melee slam +4 (1d4+1), touch +4 (2 plus energy drain)

Special Attacks energy drain (one level, DC 15)

Spell-Like Abilities (CL 5th; concentration +8)

At will—*possession* (DC 18)

Str —, **Dex** 13, **Con** —, **Int** 13, **Wis** 12, **Cha** 17

Base Atk +3; **CMB** +4; **CMD** 17

Feats Combat Expertise, Combat Reflexes, Stand Still

Skills Disguise +11, Knowledge (arcana) +9, Knowledge (religion) +9, Perception +9, Sense Motive +9

Languages Common, Necronomus

SQ rejuvenation

Special Abilities

Rejuvenation (Su) A slain chi thief mogwai returns to unlife at full hit points at the next sundown. On the anniversary of its wrongful death, a chi thief mogwai reforms 1 hour after it is reduced to 0 hit points. The only way to destroy a chi thief mogwai is to bring to light the true offender or lay the spirit to rest with a ritual.

Niu Tian Shen

Corporeal Form

A massive, obviously wounded ox. The ox is missing one of its horns. He is almost twice the size of a standard ox. The slobber and snot coming from his nose and mouth are a grayish-green ichor.

Niu Tian Shen   CR 8

XP 4,800
NG Huge outsider (kami, native)
Init -1; **Senses** darkvision 60 ft., low-light vision, scent; Perception +11
AC 20, touch 7, flat-footed 20 (-1 Dex, +13 natural, -2 size)
hp 101 (8d10+56); fast healing 4
Fort +8, **Ref** +5, **Will** +6
DR 5/magic and silver; **Immune** bleed, mind-affecting effects, petrification, polymorph; **Resist** acid 10, electricity 10, fire 10
Speed 40 ft.
Melee gore +18 (3d6 + 18 plus 1d6 acid)
Space 15 ft.; **Reach** 10 ft.
Special Attacks acid (1d6 acid), trample (3d6 + 18, DC 26)
Str 35, **Dex** 8, **Con** 23, **Int** 13, **Wis** 11, **Cha** 14
Base Atk +8; **CMB** +22 (+24 bull rush); **CMD** 31 (33 vs. bull rush, 35 vs. trip)
Feats Endurance, Improved Bull Rush, Power Attack, Toughness
Skills Acrobatics -1 (+3 to jump), Knowledge (local) +9, Knowledge (nature) +9, Knowledge (planes) +12, Perception +11, Perform (wind instruments) +10, Profession (farmer) +8, Sense Motive +11
Languages Celestial, Common; telepathy 100 ft.
SQ merge with ward
Special Abilities
Merge with Ward (Su) As a standard action, a kami can merge its body and mind with its ward. When merged, the kami can observe the surrounding region with its senses as if it were using its own body, as well as via any senses its ward might have. It has no control over its ward, nor can it communicate or otherwise take any action other than to emerge from its ward as a standard action. A kami must be adjacent to its ward to merge with or emerge from it. If its ward is a creature, plant, or object, the kami can emerge mounted on the creature provided the kami's body is at least one size category smaller than the creature. If its ward is a location, the kami may emerge at any point within that location.

Incorporeal Form

Niu Tian Shen is unable to manifest in corporeal form at this time. The zhenniao poison affected his mind and left him maddened, running on primal instinct.

Niu Tian Shen (incorporeal form)   CR 6

XP 2,400
NG Large outsider (incorporeal, kami, native)
Init +0; **Senses** darkvision 60 ft., low-light vision, scent; Perception +11
AC 17, touch 9, flat-footed 17 (+8 natural, -1 size)
hp 85 (8d10+40); fast healing 4
Fort +6, **Ref** +6, **Will** +6
Immune bleed, mind-affecting effects, petrification, polymorph; **Resist** acid 10, electricity 10, fire 10
Speed 40 ft.
Melee gore +15 (2d6 + 12 plus 1d6 acid)
Space 10 ft.; **Reach** 5 ft.
Special Attacks trample (2d6 + 12 plus 1d6 acid, DC 22)
Str 27, **Dex** 10, **Con** 19, **Int** 13, **Wis** 11, **Cha** 14
Base Atk +8; **CMB** +17 (+19 bull rush); **CMD** 27 (29 vs. bull rush, 31 vs. trip)
Feats Endurance, Improved Bull Rush, Power Attack, Toughness
Skills Acrobatics +0 (+4 to jump), Knowledge (local) +9, Knowledge (nature) +9, Knowledge (planes) +12, Perception +11, Perform (wind instruments) +10, Profession (farmer) +8, Sense Motive +11
Languages Celestial, Common; telepathy 100 ft.
SQ merge with ward
Special Abilities
Merge with Ward (Su) As a standard action, a kami can merge its body and mind with its ward. When merged, the kami can observe the surrounding region with its senses as if it were using its own body, as well as via any senses its ward might have. It has no control over its ward, nor can it communicate or otherwise take any action other than to emerge from its ward as a standard action. A kami must be adjacent to its ward to merge with or emerge from it. If its ward is a creature, plant, or object, the kami can emerge mounted on the creature provided the kami's body is at least one size category smaller than the creature. If its ward is a location, the kami may emerge at any point within that location.

Underworld Phantasms

Underworld Phantasms are incorporeal beings condemned to wander the underworld. Once awakened, they want to stay and hope to use the characters to achieve that goal.

They are translucent, with pale and tortured features. Their hair flows loosely back, and their eyes are hollow.

They try to possess a character and use that being to attack the others. If that doesn't work, they wail, causing sonic damage.

Underworld Phantasm   CR 9

XP 6,400
CE Medium undead (incorporeal)
Init +9; **Senses** darkvision 60 ft.; Perception +21
AC 18, touch 18, flat-footed 13 (+3 deflection, +5 Dex)
hp 90 (12d8+36)
Fort +9, **Ref** +9, **Will** +10
Defensive Abilities incorporeal; **Immune** undead traits
Speed fly 60 ft. (perfect)
Melee touch +15 (1d6 + 2 plus energy drain)
Special Attacks energy drain (one level, DC 19), piercing scream (6d6 sonic damage, once every 1d4 rounds), possession
Spell-Like Abilities (CL 12th; concentration +15)
3/day—*charm person* (DC 16)
Str —, **Dex** 21, **Con** —, **Int** 15, **Wis** 15, **Cha** 16
Base Atk +9; **CMB** +14; **CMD** 27
Feats Ability Focus (charm person), Alertness, Blind-fight, Great Fortitude, Improved Initiative, Weapon Focus (touch attack)
Skills Bluff +15, Fly +28, Intimidate +18, Perception +21, Sense Motive +21, Stealth +20
Languages Abyssal, Common, Necronomus
Special Abilities
Piercing Scream (DC 19) (Su) Every 1d4 rounds, deal 6d6 sonic damage to creatures in 60-ft cone (Fort half).
Possession (DC 19) (Su) Once per round, by making a successful incorporeal touch attack, a phantasm can merge its body with a creature on the Material Plane. This ability is similar to a magic jar spell, except that it doesn't require a receptacle. If the attack succeeds, the phantasm's body vanishes into the opponent's body. The target can resist the attack with a successful Will save (DC 21). A creature that successfully saves is immune to that phantasm's possession ability for one day.
A possessing phantasm automatically deals one negative level (from its energy drain ability) each round. A possessed creature can attempt a Will save (DC 19) each round to force the phantasm out of its body. If successful, the phantasm is ejected from the host and cannot attempt to possess the same host for 1 minute. If turned or subjected to a dismissal spell while possessing a host, the phantasm is likewise ejected. The save DCs are Charisma-based.

About the Author

Alice is a Chinese-American born and raised in the San Francisco Bay area of California. Both her parents fled from China to Taiwan at very young ages and later emigrated to America. Growing up the oldest of two children, Alice was taught to speak Mandarin at home and English outside the home. While at home, she listened to tapes and watched Chinese TV shows about Sun[1] Wu[4]kong[1] (The Monkey King), Feng[1] Shen[2] Bang[4] (Creation of the Gods/Investiture of the Gods), and many stories about magic and mythology from the Chinese culture. This imbued her with a strong passion for the genre and culture. She hopes to give a glimpse into the epic craziness of a world where gods and immortals constantly meddle and involve themselves in the everyday lives of mankind.

Alice has been a pen & paper gamer since the late '90s and is a true polygamer. Every genre and system she can get exposure to, she tries to experience. She tries to experience games of every genre and system, from the crunch-heavy Hero System to the system light Ghost Echo. She's played more than 200 games, and that number continues to climb. Alice is a host of the Babies with Knives podcast that focuses on teaching a variety of tabletop roleplaying games.

NECROMANCER
Games™